KU-137-742

Jane Porter grew up on a diet of Mills & Boon®
romances, reading late at night under the covers
so her mother wouldn't see! She wrote her first
book at age eight, and spent many of her school
and college years living abroad, immersing
herself in other cultures and continuing to read
voraciously. Now Jane has settled down in rugged
Seattle, Washington, with her gorgeous husband
and two sons. Jane loves to hear from her readers.
You can write to her at PO Box 524, Bellevue,
WA 98009, USA. Or visit her website at
www.janeporter.com

For my posse, the great girls
who got me through it all—
Kelly, Lori, Lisa, Kristina, Cheryl,
Sinclair, Joan, Janie & Janette. I love you.

PROLOGUE

FORCE a girl to marry?

Take her from her home? Carry her hostage across the Atlantic Ocean? Isolate her from family and friends until she finally caved, acquiescing to her father's desire that she marry...even if the man were twenty years older?

Sheikh Kalen Tarq Nuri had heard worse.

Draining his martini, he pushed the empty glass away, black eyebrows flattening over narrowed eyes.

He was in New York having closed a big deal and was now out to dinner celebrating the acquisition with his top brass, those who'd executed the nasty buyout. The other company hadn't wanted to be bought. Sheikh Nuri had wanted the purchase.

Sheikh Nuri got what he wanted. Always.

Tapping the rim of his empty martini glass, Kalen Nuri felt a surge of desire, the desire of a hunter, the desire of a predator. Like the hawks he used to own in Baraka, the beautiful fierce falcons, Kalen was ready to hunt.

To give chase.

To pounce.

There were worse things than forcing a young woman to marry against her will.

There was betrayal. Attempted murder. And the revelation of a plot to assassinate not just the Sultan of Baraka, but the Sultan's young sons. Kalen's nephews.

Sheikh Kalen Nuri's jaw hardened, eyes narrowing to slits of masked rage. No one touched his family. No one would be allowed to hurt Malik or the children. *No one.* Not even Omar al-Issidri, his brother's chief cabinet member. Secret agitator.

Kalen had learned that Omar had plans, big plans, plans to consolidate his power in Baraka by marrying his daughter to Ahmed Abizhaid, a radical fundamentalist. A man that also happened to be the Sultan's harshest critic.

Omar was dangerous because he was weak. Ahmed was dangerous because he was violent. The two together could destroy the Nuris. But Malik, honest, honorable, noble Malik, refused to believe that Omar was anything less than a dedicated public servant.

Kalen's fingers tightened around the stem of the martini glass. The marriage between twenty-three-year-old Keira al-Issidri and Ahmed Abizhaid couldn't take place. It was a dangerous relationship, an alliance that would give Ahmed respectability and access to the palace. As well as proximity to the Sultan and his children.

Which is why Kalen hadn't wanted the marriage to take place.

And then someone made a mistake. Botched the job. Someone had let him down.

It infuriated Kalen. If the situation had been handled correctly, everything would have been sorted, settled, the problem contained.

Instead Keira al-Issidri would be flying back to Baraka tomorrow night and into her new bridegroom's bed.

Unless Kalen did something about it immediately. Which was why Kalen had to make arrangements to ensure the marriage didn't take place. Personally. And given the circumstances, it was exactly what Kalen intended to do.

CHAPTER ONE

SHE'D like to start it all over if she could.

She'd like to rewind the tape to the place where it all went wrong. That night. The party. The week she'd turned sixteen.

If she'd never disobeyed her father…

If she'd never snuck out to attend something forbidden…

If she'd never gone where good Barakan girls shouldn't go…

But that was all years ago and this was now and Keira Gordon's fingers felt nerveless as they wrapped tightly around the telephone. "I'm not marrying him. I can't marry him, Father. It's impossible."

Omar al-Issidri drew a short, impatient breath. "The only thing impossible is that you're twenty-three and still single! You're shaming our family, you're shaming our name."

Keira knew in Baraka young women married early to protect their reputations, but Keira wasn't Barakan. She'd never been Barakan. But she wasn't

English, either, despite having spent the majority of her life in Manchester with her liberal, intellectual mother.

"He's a prominent man, Keira. Connected, powerful, influential—"

"I don't care."

Silence stretched across the phone line. "You must understand, Keira, that this is important. It's important for all of us. You need to marry. Sidi Abizhaid has chosen you. You should be flattered by his interest."

Her father wasn't listening to a thing she said. But according to her mother, her father never did listen to anyone, at least not to any woman, which was only one of the reasons her mother had left him all those years ago.

Keira rubbed her forehead. She cared about her father, she did, but her father had no idea how Western she was, how removed she'd become from the veiled life of Baraka, a North African kingdom filled with rose tinted mountains, golden sand dunes and beautiful port cities more European than Middle Eastern. "I live in Dallas, Father. I have a job here. I have wonderful friends here, people who really care about me—"

"But no husband."

"I don't want a husband." Exasperation sharpened

her voice. "I've barely finished school, haven't even begun to establish myself in my career."

"Career?"

"Yes. I want a career. I've a good brain—"

"This is your mother's doing. I should have never allowed her to take you out of the country. I should have kept you here, with me. She wasn't fit to be a parent."

Overwhelmed by a rush of anger, Keira bit her tongue. Both of her parents had played games, both had used her in a vicious tug-of-war between them.

"Marriage is an honor," her father added now. "And a good marriage would bring honor to all of us."

Not to me, she answered silently, savagely, feeling a rise of fierce emotion, the emotion tied to memories so old it was as if they'd been with her always. "I've no desire to marry," she repeated, voice strangled. "It's not something I've ever wished for myself."

"But it's something I've wished for you. You are my only child. You are my future."

"No."

He made a rough sound, part irritation part anger. "Don't shame me, Keira al-Issidri. Do not shame the family." The warning was clear and while she felt her father's frustration, there was nothing she could do about it. She could never be what he wanted her to be.

She could only be herself. And what she was, who she'd become, was unacceptable in Baraka.

But her father didn't know... Her father would never know.

With a glance at her wristwatch, she noted the late hour, felt a twinge of panic at the thought of the traffic if she didn't leave immediately. "I have to go. I can't be late for work."

"Work? What work do you do on a Sunday morning?"

One more thing her father didn't know about her. It seemed her father knew nothing about who she really was. "I dance."

Critical silence stretched across the phone line. Her father had never approved of her ballet training but his opposition had grown worse as she hit adolescence. When she turned twelve he wanted the classes to stop but she wouldn't. And then a year later when he discovered she didn't just take lessons with boys at the Royal Ballet School, but performed on stage as Clara in a Christmas production of the *Nutcracker*, he'd threatened to return her to Baraka. Immediately. Permanently.

No daughter of his would wear a leotard and tights in public.

No daughter of his would be touched—even if

partnered in a pas de deux—by a member of the opposite sex.

And her mother, always defiant, never intimidated, had crumbled.

It was her mother, her fierce rebel radical mother, who made Keira stop dancing. *You don't want to antagonize your father. He isn't like us. He could do anything if provoked...*

After eight years of daily lessons at the school, after years of loving, living, breathing ballet, after eight years where the smooth hardwood floors, the smell of rosin, the slippery satin of her pale pink pointe shoe ribbons, the intense discipline of barre work before floor work were more familiar than her own home, she'd dropped her lessons. Like that.

"I thought you gave up your dancing," her father said now.

"I did," Keira answered softly. And it had killed her. Broken her heart. But her mother wouldn't relent and her father had been pleased and it was just another example of the way her parents had warred. What she wanted, *needed,* hadn't ever figured in the equation. Her parents' fights and decisions were based on their personal agendas. Their own ambition. And both had been hugely, voraciously ambitious.

"I do have to go," she added, knowing that nothing

her father could say would change her mind. In America she'd finally found peace—acceptance—and there was no way in hell she'd ever return to Baraka.

It wasn't that Baraka wasn't beautiful, or the mix of cultures—Berber, Bedouin, Arab and European—hadn't created a fascinating landscape of language and customs. But in Baraka, women were still protected, sheltered, segregated, and she'd spent too many years in England and America to ever live that way again.

"Keira, you cannot ignore your responsibility."

She felt a weight settle on her, felt the cultural differences between them stretch, vast, unapproachable, endless. "I'm sorry, but I don't believe in arranged marriages. I don't find it acceptable, even if most Barakan girls do."

Heavy silence stretched between them. At last Omar al-Issidri spoke. "Twenty-four hours, Keira. That's all I give you."

"No."

"I'm not asking. I'm telling you. You will return within twenty-four hours or I will have you returned to me." And he hung up.

For a moment Keira could only stare at the phone before slowly hanging up. Her father couldn't be serious. He couldn't intend to drag her forcibly home…

Numbly she gathered her duffel bag and purse and headed for her car. Her hands shook on the steering wheel as she drove to the football stadium in thick game day traffic. Marry someone she didn't know? Marry a Barakan leader just because her father said so?

With one eye on traffic and the other on her mobile phone's keypad, she punched in her father's phone number.

"I can't believe you're serious," she said as soon as her father answered. "I can't believe you'd threaten me with such a thing. I've never lived in Baraka. I haven't visited in seven years—"

"Yet you are Barakan whether you admit it or not. And I've been patient with you. I've allowed you to conclude your studies in the States, but you've finished your coursework, it's time you came home."

"Baraka isn't my home!" She quickly shifted down the gears, coming to a stop as the heavy traffic ground to a standstill turning the four-lane highway into a sea of red brake lights.

"You were born in Atiq. You spent your childhood here."

"Until I was four." And yes, she might have been born in the coastal city of Atiq, the sprawling capital of Baraka, where the buildings were all whitewashed, and the streets narrow and winding, but she was English, not Barakan. And her memories of Baraka were the memories of a visitor, a guest, memories generated from her annual visit to her father's home.

Growing up, Keira had dreaded the trip to her father's each summer. The annual visit became increasingly fraught with tension as she went from childhood to adolescence. Every year meant fewer freedoms, less opportunity to socialize, to be herself. Instead her father was determined to mold her into the perfect Barakan woman—beautiful, skilled, *silent*.

"I will never return," she said now, speaking slowly in English, and then switching to Arabic for her father's benefit. "I would rather die than return."

For a long moment her father said nothing and then his voice came across the phone, his voice hard and cold like the thick sheets of ice that covered the lakes in the North. "Be careful what you wish for." And he hung up.

Again.

Omar al-Issidri would not be happy to know how his daughter spent her free time.

Sheikh Kalen Nuri watched the queue of beautiful young women rush through the dark stadium tunnel out onto the sunny field for the half-time show.

Music blared from stadium loud speakers and Kalen Nuri watched the beautiful girls, all sleek arms and legs, skin enticingly revealed, tight tops that jutted perfect breasts, tiny white short shorts, knee high white boots, dance in formation. High kicks. Thrusting hips. Shoulders shifting, breasts jiggling.

Kalen's gaze swept the rows of young women, bypassing the many honey-blondes for the brunette in the back row, her seductively long hair the color of obsidian and reaching the small of her back. Keira al-Issidri. Omar's daughter.

Kalen's lips compressed. Keira al-Issidri must have a death wish. Omar had been livid when his only daughter left the United Kingdom four years ago to study in the States. England was bad. America far worse.

What would Omar do if he knew his daughter was shaking more than just her blue, white and silver pom poms before sixty thousand people?

Keira al-Issidri was in serious trouble. In more ways than one.

It might be late September, Keira thought out on the playing field, but it felt like the hottest day of summer.

In the middle of the grass, beneath the blinding

hot Texas sun, Keira's head spun as she kicked and twirled and shimmied, her short shorts riding high on her thighs, her white boots clinging to her calves as she kicked her leg up over her head.

She was going to be ill.

But it wasn't the hot sun making Keira her sick. It was the realization that she didn't know her father, she'd never known her father, and that if her father was determined to do as he'd vowed, there was nowhere she could go to hide from him, no way to escape.

Her father had too much money. Too many connections. Her father, the Sultan's right-hand man, had all of Baraka's resources at his disposal. If he wanted her home. He'd get her home.

Chest tightening, air bottled inside her lungs, Keira tried to force herself to concentrate on the dance routine but she couldn't escape her father's voice, or the memory of his threat, and as the sun beat onto her skull like a hammer on a drum, she felt a strange disconnection with the rest of her body. Her legs were lifting, kicking, her arms moving, her body spinning, bending.

Lifting her face to the sun, Keira let the hot golden rays cover her and tried to block the sickening knowledge that pounded in her brain.

Things were about to get ugly.

Very, very ugly.

Hours after the game ended Keira leaned on the railing of a penthouse balcony holding a glass of wine she wasn't drinking.

She hadn't wanted to come to the party tonight, hadn't been in the mood to socialize with a bunch of people she didn't know, but one of the owners of the team had invited her, told her he had an important guest in town, and he hoped Keira would attend the party he was giving for his guest.

The team owner—who was also the man who wrote her paychecks—rarely asked anything of her and Keira reluctantly showered, dressed and headed to the party.

Now she stood on the balcony, which was blessedly dark, fixed her gaze on the lights of downtown Dallas, and tried to relax. But her father's threat usurped every other thought. He'd vowed to drag her home. Vowed to force her into this marriage.

What was she going to do? Where could she go? For that matter, who could she go to?

Her father had served the Sultan of Baraka for fourteen years—nearly all of the Sultan's reign. Her father had power, connections, wealth. He inspired fear in those who crossed him.

Who would help her, knowing her father was Omar al-Issidri? Who would take such a risk with his or her life?

She frowned faintly, rubbed at her temple. It hurt

to think. It'd been such an ungodly long day and now she was here, trapped on the balcony, assaulted by the rock music pulsing from speakers inside the apartment and the raucous laughter of rich men seducing beautiful women.

She shouldn't have come. The music was too hard, too loud. The people too different. The night too hot and humid.

She was tired. Overwhelmed. Panic set in. This was not a good place to be, not safe for her, not safe in any way. Clutching her wineglass, she drew a deep breath, and then another. *Calm, think calm. Nothing bad is going to happen. Everything's fine.*

It had been years and she still hated parties. All these years and the heat, the noise, the liquor-fueled gaiety of parties still unnerved her. You could run from the past, she thought wearily, but the past eventually caught up.

"Don't jump." A male voice, cool and mocking, spoke behind her. His accent was different— British, cultured, and yet exotic.

Keira felt the strangest prickle at the back of her neck, but she didn't turn around. "I've no intention of jumping," she answered equally coolly, lifting her wineglass and taking a sip while keeping her gaze fixed on the skyline.

"Even though you're hopelessly trapped?"

She beat back the flicker of alarm. Ignored the silver slide of adrenaline. "A bit presumptuous, don't you think?"

"Not if you know as much about someone as I know about you."

She didn't like his tone, or his cocky attitude. Arrogant men turned her off. And while her survival instinct told her to race back to the penthouse, she wasn't about to give the man the pleasure of watching her run like a timid jackrabbit.

"I could call your bluff," she said, giving her glass a swirl, "but I don't care enough to continue this conversation."

"Then I shall call your bluff, *Lalla* Keira al-Issidri."

Arabic. And not just Arabic, but Barakan Arabic.

He knew her father. He had to know her father. He'd called her Keira al-Issidri.

Slowly, painfully, she forced herself to turn to face him but the shadows darkened the balcony just like the shadows filling her head. "Who are you?"

"A family friend."

Her lashes closed, her breath failing. It had happened already. Her father had sent someone for her. Her father hadn't waited twenty-four hours. He hadn't even waited eight hours.

She opened her eyes, drew a deep breath to settle her nerves. "What do you want?"

"To give you options."

She trusted no man, least of all a Barakan male. "I don't understand you."

"I think you do."

There was something in his tone that made her nerves scream, a familiarity that didn't sit right at all with her. "Step into the light," she said crisply, investing as much authority into her voice as she could manage. "I want to see you."

"Why?"

"I want to see the cowardly man that enjoys intimidating a woman."

"In that case." He moved from the shadows, toward the yellow light pouring through the open glass door.

"Better?" he drawled, hands shoved in his trouser pockets. "Can you see the cowardly man now?"

She inhaled sharply, eyes widening in shock. She shied away from who—what—she saw.

"Perhaps the shadows are better," he said, moving away from the doorway again, slowly walking toward her.

"Yes. That way you can do whatever it is you want to do."

"And what do I want to do?" he sounded mildly intrigued.

"Drag me back to Baraka."

"Ah."

That one sound was strangely beautiful, seductive, conjuring a sailing ship carrying precious cargo of gold and spices from faraway places.

He stopped not far from her, took a position at the balcony railing, leaned against the smooth polished steel.

In the dark with the help of the faraway moon, she tried to make out his face and shape. In the reflection of ghostly white light she saw straight black eyebrows, the high hard edge of cheekbone, a strong uncompromising jaw.

The line of cheekbone and jaw was familiar. Too familiar although it'd been years since she saw the one, the dream...the one, true fantasy...

She closed her eyes, not wanting to remember, the association too tangled with heartbreak and pain. No dream should be so abruptly broken, not the way she'd been broken.

Keira drew another breath, opened her eyes, and yet without looking at him, she was uncomfortably aware of him, aware of his size, his height, the length of his long legs. "My father didn't even wait twenty-four hours." It was impossible to hide her bitterness. "He'd said he'd give me twenty-four hours. He lied."

There was a moment's silence. She could have

sworn he smiled and then he said, "I'm not your father's emissary."

She could barely breathe. Her head felt even woozier than before. It was a strange terror filling her. "Then who the hell are you?"

"You don't remember me?"

He asked the question so softly that it did something terrible to her. Took her heart, her chest, her lungs and mashed them into a bitter ball.

She knew who he was, she'd known from the moment he spoke but she hadn't wanted to believe it, couldn't believe it. Not after all these years.

"I'm certain you remember me," he added.

Ice filled her veins, blocks of ice that clashed wildly with the rush of blood to her face. "Go back to the light."

"You're being silly."

And then he struck a match, and in the small bright yellow flame, she saw him. Clearly. And she stared hard at the face opposite her, stared directly, determined to see what she wouldn't let herself see before.

Not just straight black eyebrows, and high hard cheekbones, but black fringed eyes that shone amber-gold.

The match burned out. Keira looked away, flattened. She wanted to shake her head, shake away the vision that burned her eyes, her mind, burned into her all of the time.

She might be able to forget his brow, his cheekbone, his jaw, but she'd never forget his eyes. Amber-gold eyes.

Amber-gold eyes surrounded by long dense black lashes. Eyes that didn't smile. Eyes that just stared through one, all the way to the heart, all the way to the soul.

No one had eyes like that. No one had ever looked at her the way he did. No one but Kalen Nuri.

Her own childish desert fantasy.

Inexplicable tears scalded the back of her eyes and she gripped her wineglass tightly. How terribly infatuated she used to be...

What a silly crush it'd been...

"Sheikh Nuri," she breathed his name, unable to look at him.

His dark head inclined, his expression blank. *"S-salamu alikum."*

The traditional Barakan greeting, *Peace on you.*

The wrong answer from what had once been the right man.

Her lips parted, air slipped out. Kalen Nuri was here. Stood just a foot away. The shock returned, hit her hard, a blow to the breastbone, a fierce punch that knocked the air from her, making her head light, nerves taut, everything too wobbly.

It had been years since she last saw him…and now he was here but he wasn't her friend. Of that much she was certain.

"You can't tell me that my father didn't send you." Her words were terse, anger pitching her voice low. "You can't lie to me, too."

He shrugged. "I can tell you the truth. But it's your choice whether to listen. Your choice what to believe."

"I want the truth."

"I know what your father intends for you."

He wasted no time, said it so bluntly that she couldn't look away, and as she stared at him the craziest things happened inside her—inarticulate words like you're here, you're really here—even as her rational mind told her that he was more dangerous than anything her father had arranged for her. "My father works for your brother."

Kalen made a dismissive gesture. "Your father works for himself."

Her eyes narrowed. "You don't trust my father."

"No." The sheikh studied her just as intently as she had examined him. "Do you trust your father?"

"He's my father."

"Youthful naiveté."

"Naiveté?"

"It's a kinder word than stupidity."

Her surge of temper didn't help the pounding that had begun at the top of her skull. "What do you want?"

"As I said, to give you options."

She said nothing, just stared at him.

Sheikh Nuri's mouth curved but the shape wasn't kind. "You don't have to marry Mr. Abizhaid."

Something inside her twisted up tight. No, she thought silently mocking herself. I used to want to marry you. "Really? And what's wrong with Ahmed Abizhaid?"

"He's old, he's hairy, he's heavyset."

"So?"

"He has children from his first marriage older than you."

She said nothing.

"He's notorious for his fanaticism."

Keira grit her teeth together, refusing to speak. She sensed that Sheikh Nuri was enjoying himself at her expense.

"And he has questionable political ambitions." The sheikh lifted his hands, an expressive gesture of laying the facts out for her. "But if this is appealing…"

His voice drifted off and she looked away, saw the lights of the city flicker, the distant white and red streams of light indicating the freeway traffic. "It's not appealing, and you know it."

"You need my help."

"I don't want your help." She didn't want anything from any man. Once she'd been trusting, once, yes, she'd been naive, but she wasn't the foolish girl of the past.

"So you'll cut off your nose to spite your face?"

"You know nothing about my nose, or my face, Sheikh Nuri."

"I know that lovely face will be veiled and hidden if you don't allow me to help."

She couldn't answer. Terror filled her. She knew the life Sheikh Nuri described, knew of the women's quarters, the secret women's world and she didn't want it. Couldn't bear it. She'd never been Barakan. She'd finished university with honors, had been hired as a communications director for Sanford Oil and Gas, an international firm based in Dallas, and she traveled, worked, succeeded. Succeeded beyond her wildest expectations.

How could she have her freedom stripped? How could she go back to what she'd escaped?

No. No. She wouldn't be segregated. Wouldn't be veiled. Would never allow herself to be hidden as though she were something to be ashamed of. "I haven't lived in Baraka since I was four," she said.

"Your father has already sent people for you."

Keira went hot, then cold.

"There are three men waiting at your house this very moment." He paused, let his words sink in. "They're not going away without you."

"I won't go home then."

"Your father has infinite resources. He'll find you wherever you go. And there his men will be. Waiting."

"No."

"Yes. And you know it's true."

She closed her eyes, hating him, hating the words he said. He was right. She knew he was right. Her father got what he wanted. Her father always did.

"Face the truth, Miss al-Issidri. It's me. Or them. Pick your poison."

CHAPTER TWO

PICK her poison?

Her father, or him? Disgusted, she groaned inwardly, her body seething with tension. "I'm not playing this game, Sheikh Nuri."

"Maybe you aren't, but your father is. Three men are waiting at your house now. They've a car, a plane, a flight plan. You go home and you become theirs."

Her disgust intensified, as did her fear. Thoroughly chilled, she craved a wrap to keep her warm. "Why should I believe you?"

"Why should I lie to you?"

He sounded so perfectly reasonable and yet none of this made sense. She hadn't lived in Baraka for years. She'd had little contact with her father these past seven years. Why would he force her into an arranged marriage now?

And what about her father's plans would bring Sheikh Nuri to her doorstep?

This was about business or economics, she thought, and she wanted no part in either.

"You've ulterior reasons for being here," she said, glancing over her shoulder at the party still in full swing. Sheikh Nuri was one of the richest, most powerful men in the world. He was the special guest. He was the reason her boss wanted her here tonight.

"Yes."

"You wanted me here tonight, didn't you?"

"You're the only reason I'm here." He extended an arm in her direction. "Shall we go and take care of business?"

She looked at him, the dim moonlight playing across the hard features of his face, and suddenly she felt sixteen again. Head over heels in love with a man easily ten years her senior and she knew their lives were so different but she wanted part of his world anyway.

"Business?" she repeated numbly, and for a moment she was that sixteen-year-old, the one who felt so painfully alienated in school, so dark and foreign compared to the beautiful English roses, the one that missed her ballet classes, the intensely disciplined world of dance, the one who never shared what she felt with anyone but kept all her secrets buried deep in her heart.

"The men invading your home."

Sheikh Nuri had a car waiting. The interior of

the car was dark, the tinted windows allowing little exterior light to penetrate.

She practically hugged the corner of her seat, her hand wrapped convulsively around the door handle.

Small spaces, dark spaces made her skin crawl and it took all of her concentration to keep from breaking into a cold sweat.

Nothing bad is going to happen…

You're just getting a ride home…

But she shouldn't have left her car at the stadium. If she hadn't left her car she'd be driving herself home. She'd be feeling safer. More secure. She wouldn't be sitting so close to a man she didn't know anymore…not that she ever really knew him. But she'd imagined.

Those fantasies.

They rode in silence and then Kalen rolled the window down. "We're almost to your neighborhood, aren't we?"

In the dark Keira could see flashes of her neighborhood, a suburb of tidy blocks with neat little houses and groomed little gardens. In the front yards of each house pink and white and purple crepe myrtles still bloomed and the first of the Japanese maple had started to turn red.

Indian summer.

Her favorite time of year.

"Yes." With one finger tip she traced the glass. She loved her little house, loved the hammock slung up in the backyard, loved the idea of owning something of her own, something that no one could take away.

And like that, they were there, reaching her quiet street with the dogwoods and Japanese maples and crepe myrtles she so loved.

"Your house," he said, slowing the car, drawing to a stop in front of her house.

"Yes." Heartbreak wrapped around her chest, tight, viselike. Was her freedom over? Slowly she turned her head, looked at Kalen Nuri intently. "Tell me again, tell me you're not an emissary for my father."

"I'm not an emissary for your father."

She didn't miss the faint mocking note in his voice, nor the strength he exuded just sitting there. There was nothing rough or rustic about Kalen Nuri, just a strength she couldn't place and the sense of power, unlimited power...

He could have been the Sultan. He could have worn the crown easily. If it weren't for the fact that his brother Malik was first born, Kalen Nuri could have been king. He was certainly proud enough. Confident enough.

"But you've spoken to my father?" she persisted, dazzled by the gold in his eyes, seeing the gilded grains of desert sand beneath the blaze of North African sun.

"No." The corners of his eyes creased. "There's little love lost between your father and me. He's forced to tolerate me because I am Malik's brother, but I dislike him intensely. And he knows it." A deep groove formed next to Kalen's mouth. "And I am here because he would not like it."

His words were met by silence, but there was nothing quiet between them, nothing still about the night. The night crackled with tension, electricity, like a dark sky before a storm but tonight the sky was clear. Just moon, and stars and beneath the moon and stars the tension grew.

Being near him like this, talking so, made her head spin, her body hum. She fought to clear her mind now. "You said I had to pick my poison."

"Yes."

"You, or them, you said."

"I did."

"Why are those my only two options?"

For a moment he didn't speak and then his broad shoulders shifted, a careless shrug. "Because who else will take on your father? Who else will turn his world inside out to prevent this marriage from taking place?"

She was missing something, there was a piece to this puzzle she didn't see, didn't understand, and she desperately wanted to understand. "I don't want a man," she said after a moment. "I do not need a man."

"Want and need are two different things. You might not want me, Miss al-Issidri, but you need me." He paused for emphasis. "There are worse things than accepting my protection."

"You mean like being forced home to marry Mr. Abizhaid?" Hot brittle laughter formed in her chest. "I think I'd rather handle this my way," she said, reaching for the door handle. "Unlock the car. I'm getting out."

She heard the doors unlock. "And you do know you have visitors in the house?" he answered calmly.

Three, he'd said and she glanced at the house but saw nothing amiss, just the light left on in the entry hall that she always left burning when she knew she'd return late. "I see no one."

"They're not going to hang a Welcome Home sign, *laeela*."

Laeela. Darling, love. An Arabic endearment that was like the kiss of the silken Saharan sands. No one had ever called her *laeela* before.

"I'll keep that in mind." She swung the door open, stepped out, slammed the door shut. "Thanks for the lift, Sheikh Nuri."

The sedan's door opened again just as quickly as Keira shut it. "You need my help."

"No," she said, backing away, "I need my car. If you really want to help me, help me get my car back from the stadium parking lot. That way I can get to work in the morning."

He laughed softly, approached her even as she continued backing away. "You really think you're going to work tomorrow?"

There was danger in his voice, a soft warning she couldn't ignore and she stopped moving long enough to meet his gaze, hold it.

There was nothing threatening in his expression but there was something else.

Knowledge.

Cynicism.

Mistrust.

Despite his dark tailored coat and the expensive leather shoes on his feet, he was a man with the sun and the wind and the desert in his eyes. More Berber than Western. Sheikh not European.

He was everything she didn't know, everything she'd never understood. Keira turned, took a panicked step toward her house, and then another, and another until she was running up the porch to the front door. Her front door swung open so abruptly that Keira barely had time to register the man standing in the doorway—her doorway—before he opened his arms and grabbed her, thick arms enfolding her.

It happened so fast she didn't even scream. One minute she was running for shelter and the next she was imprisoned and her mind went dark, blank, the blank from years past when terror was too great, when physical pain overrode mental pain and everything went quiet. Still.

Helplessly she turned her head, looked toward the brick walkway and Sheikh Nuri was there. Watching.

If only someone had been able to help her. If only someone had done something. If only someone...

You're not sixteen. You're a woman. Fight, Keira, fight.

And finally her vocal cords opened and she screamed. She wouldn't die, wouldn't fade to nothing this time. She wasn't going to disappear, wouldn't become air and light, wouldn't lose herself again.

Thrashing now, her fear turned her into a demon horse, all thunder and hooves. Then panic gave way to rage. She wasn't going to be hurt again. She'd never let herself be hurt again and her body came to life, elbows jabbing at ribs, feet kicking, aiming for knees.

"Put me down," she demanded, "put me down now. I won't go."

And still she kicked and jabbed and she knew she got her assailant at least once good and hard as she heard a soft oath from behind her, a hiss of air between clenched teeth. "I won't go," she repeated, swinging her legs wildly, trying to connect with his groin, or a knee.

Desperation laced her brain. Sheikh Nuri could stop this. He could help her. He'd said he would.

But he said nothing, he simply stood there and all she knew was that she wouldn't go back to Baraka, she wouldn't be returned to her father's house against her will.

Her desperate gaze found Sheikh Nuri's and she hated him and yet needed him and she sobbed his name. "Kalen. Kalen, help me."

It was enough. It was all he needed.

"Put her down." Kalen Nuri's coldly furious voice sliced through the air.

The man holding Keira froze. "Your Excellency."

"Put her down," Sheikh Nuri repeated, speaking Barakan, and it was a direct command from a member of the royal Nuri family. His authority was unmistakable.

"But, Your Excellency, we have been sent to bring her home."

Kalen Nuri was walking now, climbing the front

steps with a grace that masked his strength. "You dare to take my woman from me?"

Deafening silence descended. All motion ceased, all talk stopped, even Keira went weak.

"Your woman?" The man holding Keira repeated.

"*My* woman." Kalen's voice thundered low and menacing like a roll of heavy thunder across the heavens.

The arms holding Keira loosened. She felt herself lowered, placed back on her feet. The moment the arms eased from around her Keira moved to Sheikh Nuri's side.

Kalen extended an arm, but didn't touch her. "*Lalla* al-Issidri is in my protection."

"But we have been sent for her." A different man spoke, the second one to appear from the house. Somewhere was a third. "*Sidi* al-Issidri was very clear."

"Let me be just as clear," the sheikh answered with mock civility. "She is mine."

Kalen glanced at Keira and Keira felt his gaze, felt a peculiar current curl in her, heat and fear, dread and anticipation. And looking at her, his amber gaze glowing hot, possessive, he added, "Keira al-Issidri is my woman. She belongs to me."

And then the three men were gone.

Magic, Keira thought, as the men climbed into

the car and drove away. Kalen might as well have been a magician like Merlin from the days of King Arthur's court.

But it wasn't magic, it was power. And he had far too much of it.

Keira faced Kalen on the front steps as the car disappeared down the street. For a moment neither spoke. Keira stared blindly past Kalen and he made no effort to start a conversation. And yet his silence wasn't easy. She felt his anger.

"So it's begun," Sheikh Nuri said, eventually breaking the silence.

She wished she could say she didn't know what he meant. She wished she were as naive as he'd accused her of being but Keira knew exactly what Kalen meant.

What had just happened on the front porch of her house was huge.

Sheikh Nuri had just publicly challenged her father. Sheikh Nuri had usurped her father's authority. And Sheikh Nuri could, because he was third in line for the throne behind his brother and his two nephews.

Her father would be livid. Livid and humiliated.

Keira pressed a hand to her brow, pressing against the ache that had taken up residence there. She'd rejected her father. Accepted Kalen Nuri's protection. In minutes she'd turned all their lives upside down.

"I should call my father," she said, voice husky, goose bumps covering her arms.

"I'm certain he's already heard."

She gave her head a faint shake. "I should at least try to talk to him."

Kalen Nuri took a step toward her, closing the distance between them. He stared at her so long and hard that she shivered and looked away.

"He is my father, after all," she added defensively.

"And what will your call achieve?"

Keira couldn't answer and Kalen took her chin in his hand, tilted her face up to his. "What do you think you'll do?" he repeated his question impatiently. "If your father intended to listen to you, to care about your opinion, to care about your needs, he would have listened to you already."

She hated what he was saying, hated that he was right and she tried to pull away but Kalen wasn't about to let her go.

"Your father was going to use you to further his own political ambitions," he added roughly, his fingers too hard on her jaw, his tone too sharp. "To a man like your father you are merely an object, a possession to be used, bartered, traded."

Each word was worse. Each word bit and stung.

"But you're the same, aren't you, Sheikh Nuri?" Her throat was swelling closed and she had to force each syllable and sound out. "You're using me, too. You're using me to get back at my father. At least be man enough to admit it."

She heard his soft hiss at her insult. His touch changed, shifted, fingers extending from her chin to her jaw, his fingers briefly caressing the width of her jawbone.

"You lack a Barakan woman's good sense and quiet tongue," he said, his thumb slowly sweeping beneath the edge of her jaw, stirring the nerves in the most tender of skin.

Her skin flamed, nerves tightening at the maddening touch. "I'm not Barakan."

"Yet I'm beginning to think you deserve a Barakan husband. One who would teach you humility and a modicum of self-control."

She ground her teeth, temper flashing in her eyes. "Hate to disappoint you, Sheikh Nuri, but some things can't be taught."

"That's where you're wrong, *laeela*. Anything can be taught. It just takes the right teacher." A flicker of dark emotion shone in his eyes. "And you would need not just a good teacher, but a patient teacher."

A hot stinging fizz went through her veins, so

hot, so intense that her lips parted on a silent gasp of tangled pleasure and pain.

He made her feel.

He made her feel far too much. "I don't want a man." She felt wild, desperate. She'd had so many feelings for Kalen Nuri all those years ago and then everything bad happened, everything had come unglued. "I never want a man."

"You will when you meet the right man."

"There is no right man."

He gave her a long, level look. "There used to be," he said, tone pitched low, hinting at intimacy and she stiffened.

"Never."

"There was. Once." His eyes narrowed, black lashes concealing his expression. "Many, many years ago."

She closed her eyes, hiding her alarm. He was bluffing. He knew nothing.

Kalen's thumb caressed her skin, lightly, teasingly stroking from chin to the small hollow beneath her earlobe. "There is always a right man. There is always the one man that can turn a girl into a woman—"

Panting, Keira pulled away, tearing herself from his touch, his words, tearing away the web he was weaving.

This wasn't happening. This couldn't be happening.

She headed into the house, trying to put fresh distance between them and yet Sheikh Nuri followed immediately. She heard the front door shut, the lock turn. They were alone in her house.

Odd.

Heartbreaking.

And for a moment Keira held her breath, nerves taut, senses too alive.

"Pack a suitcase," Kalen said, meeting her in the hall, just outside her bedroom door. He looked so incongruous in her small, snug house with the bright yellow painted walls and the rich oak trim. It was a sunny house. A happy house. "We need to leave soon."

Pack. Leave. He was frightening her and nervously she reached up, smoothed tendrils of hair back, combing her long dark ponytail, the ebony strands falling over her shoulder. "I can't just leave. I have a job, responsibilities—"

"You chose me, remember?"

His soft question silenced her. She didn't know what to say. Nothing came to mind. Nothing about this was logical and logic was her cornerstone, her foundation. Logic was how she functioned. Logic. Order. Structure.

In her bedroom she grabbed at clothes, pulling shirts and blouses, skirts and slacks from hangers.

Everything went into her suitcase, shoes and belts and underwear, too.

She emerged ten minutes later, silent. He nodded at her suitcase, the purse in her hand, the coat over her arm. "Good. Let's go."

In the back of his car she sat as far from him as possible. She stared at a point beyond the car window. Minutes passed. Nothing was said but clearly the driver was heading somewhere. There was a definite destination in mind.

"Where are we going?" she asked, forcing herself to speak.

"London."

"London?"

"That big city in England."

Years ago she'd had a crush on Kalen Nuri, had even imagined herself in love with him. Kalen Nuri had dominated every waking thought—never mind her dreams. Now she was horrified she'd wasted one thought on him, much less a single breath. "You do not amuse me."

"Does any man amuse you?"

When she didn't answer he laughed softly, and there was nothing remotely kind in his laughter. "You're one of those man-haters, aren't you?"

"I didn't realize we'd become a species, Sheikh Nuri."

He laughed again, even more unkindly than

before. "It will be interesting having you in my protection."

"I've changed my mind."

"Too late. You're in my car. In my care."

"Stop the car."

"And soon you will travel in my airplane."

"I won't—"

"You will, because you, Keira al-Issidri, cannot stop what you have started. It has begun. This. Us—"

"No." Hysteria bubbled up, bubbling close to the surface. "I didn't know what I was doing, I wasn't thinking—"

"You knew at the time. You knew it was me, or them. You chose me."

She could hardly breathe. Her chest constricted. Her lungs felt as though they were collapsing. *Try another tactic,* a little voice urged her, *there must be another way to reach him.*

She tried again. "It's not that I don't appreciate your concern, Sheikh Nuri, but I'm twenty-three, nearing twenty-four. I live in Dallas, am employed here in Dallas, and going to London isn't possible."

Kalen Nuri said nothing.

The car continued sailing along the freeway.

Keira felt her freedom ebb.

"You're nearly as Western as I, Sheikh Nuri." She

attempted to reason with him, remind him of all that which they shared. "You've lived in London for at least fifteen years. You wouldn't treat an English woman this way, would you?"

"I would. If she'd made a promise to me."

"I made no promise!"

"But you did. You said my name, you asked for my help, and I heard you. I extended my protection to you."

"I'm an adult, Kalen—"

"There you go. Kalen. You called to me in front of your house. You used my given name then just as you did now. Kalen, you said. Help me, Kalen." Sheikh Nuri's golden gaze narrowed, fixed on her, a curious mixture of sympathy and contempt. "If you're an adult, Keira al-Issidri, you wouldn't play games like a child."

She exhaled in a slow stream, head spinning. "I don't see this as a game."

"Good. It's not."

He settled back on his seat as though he were finished. That the discussion was now closed, as if there was nothing left to be said. But there was plenty, Keira thought, plenty to still say, plenty to be decided. Like where he'd drop her off. And how he intended to get her car back to her.

"An adult," she repeated more fiercely, staring

at him pointedly. "And I don't need looking after. Especially not by a man."

That caught his attention. He turned his attention back to her. "By a man," he repeated softly, the words echoing between them. "Just what did happen to turn you off men so completely, Miss al-Issidri?"

She forced herself to meet his gaze and his expression was thoughtful, thick black lashes fringing intelligent golden eyes. Keira felt the oddest curl in her belly, a flutter of feeling that made everything inside her tense. "Nothing happened."

"Interesting."

She saw the tug of a smile at his firm lips. He had a mouth that was sensual, the lower lip fuller than the upper, and when he smiled mockingly as he did now, he looked as if he knew things that could bring a woman to her knees.

"You might be surprised to discover that there are good men out there," he added, still smiling.

His smile inspired fear. He'd taken her father on, and now he was challenging her.

He enjoyed power. Relished control. Keira blinked a little, overwhelmed by the differences between them.

Kalen might live in London, might have left Baraka well over a decade ago, and perhaps his clothes were gorgeous Italian designs, and his accent British old school, but he was still a sheikh, and not just any sheikh, but one of the richest, most influential men in the world.

His lashes lifted, his golden gaze met hers, holding her captive. He was looking at her as though she were naked, his eyes baring her, not sexually, but emotionally. He was seeing what she didn't want seen. He was seeing the shadows in her, the places of anger and defiance, and heat seeped through her. A scorching heat that started in her belly and moved to her breasts, her neck, every inch of skin.

She felt as if she were fighting for her life now. "I'm trying to be practical, Sheikh Nuri."

"Practical, how?"

"It's necessary I establish my independence from my father, that I demonstrate in his eyes, that I am not going to marry whomever he wants, just because he wants."

"Your father doesn't care."

"Nor do you."

Her flash of resentment resulted in a low rough laugh that rumbled from his chest. "So much fire, *laeela,* so much defiance. But unlike your father, I could grow to want someone like you."

CHAPTER THREE

THE jet took off an hour before midnight. It was Kalen Nuri's private jet, a brand-new aircraft waiting at the executive terminal on the outskirts of Fort Worth.

Sheikh Nuri had her shown to the private bedroom in the back even though the last thing Keira wanted to do was sleep. But later, after reaching cruising altitude, Keira did manage to stretch out on the bed and close her eyes.

And then she was being woken, informed by the flight attendant on board that they were making the final approach into the business airport adjacent to Heathrow.

On the ground, the jet taxied to the terminal. Disembarking took minutes and as the morning sun shone warmly overhead, they slipped into a private car, traveling in silence to Sheikh Nuri's home in Kensington Gardens.

"You've been exceptionally quiet," Kalen said, as the car wound through the old elegant neighborhood, a neighborhood of grand Victorian mansions, all gleaming creamy-white in the pure morning light.

"What's there for me to say?" She couldn't even bring herself to look at him. He'd forced her here, forced her to come to London as surely as her father's men would have forced her to return to Baraka.

"You'll grow to enjoy the lifestyle."

Her head snapped around, eyebrows lowering. "Please tell me you're kidding."

"No." The car stopped before a tall house with a glossy black door, iron railings at tall paned windows, the symmetry of the house more striking for the perfect boxwood topiaries framing the entrance.

He stepped out. The front door of the house opened, a butler appeared on the front step even as the uniformed chauffeur moved around to the side of the car to assist them.

"Welcome to your future," Kalen said, upper lip curling with dark humor. Sheikh Nuri's face was just as she'd always remembered—hard, perfectly symmetrical, classically beautiful—like a marble statue. His beauty was that precise. His control was that absolute.

"My future?" she repeated.

His lip curled further, emphasizing his harsh beauty. "Your life with me."

For a moment Keira could only stare at him, finding it all too incredible, too implausible for her to believe.

She, who'd been infatuated with Sheikh Nuri for so long, was in his protection.

She, Keira Gordon, was to live with the one man she'd most admired. The man she, as a schoolgirl, had secretly, passionately adored.

Inside the house, Keira paced her bedroom suite like a caged tiger.

Kalen's house. Kalen's guest bedroom. Kalen's proximity would kill her.

She still felt so hopelessly attracted to him, and she shouldn't. He might be physically beautiful but he was hard, arrogant, insensitive.

He was using her, too, using her to get to her father and yet instead of feeling contempt for him, she felt…curiosity. Desire.

She wanted contact.

Wanted warmth and nearness, wanted skin.

She stopped pacing long enough to open a closet and look inside. Empty.

Bureau drawers, empty.

Good.

Although the room was masculine, she was afraid she might be sharing another woman's bedroom, and she couldn't do that. She'd never be able to share Kalen Nuri with anyone. Funny how some things were so damn clear.

Keira sat down on the arm of an upholstered chair. So this was her room. A high white ceiling. Mushroom painted walls. The velvet headboard a dark fern-green. Two small dressers flanked the bed—both dressers mirrored—and the large pillows butting against the headboard were various shades of moss, fern and forest velvet.

Kalen's house, she silently repeated. Kalen's guest room.

Kalen.

Seven years ago she'd gone to the party to see him. Malik Nuri might be the older brother and heir to the throne, but Kalen was the Nuri all the girls were crazy about.

Kalen was the one to get.

Kalen wasn't narrow, political, boring. Kalen lived in London, traveled extensively, spent money freely, spoiling friends…including his women.

All the good girls among the Atiq upper class fantasized about being Kalen's woman. What it would mean. What life would be like.

And it wasn't even his money the girls liked. It was his attitude.

His arrogance. His cynicism. His physical beauty. For he was beautiful. Beautiful but forbidden. In Baraka it was a woman's duty to remain pure, untouched, until her marriage. Women tended to marry young to protect their name and the family reputation. But when Kalen Nuri walked into a room, and when Kalen Nuri looked at a girl—woman—even if she was wearing a jellaba, even if only her eyes were showing—he looked at her as though he owned her. Owned her heart, mind, body and soul.

He was a magician. A sorcerer.

He was mystery and danger, sensuality and power. The ultimate fantasy.

He'd been her fantasy, too.

Which is why she'd snuck out, gone with a couple of the other girls, wilder girls, girls with parents less restrictive, less conservative than her father to the party hosted in Kalen Nuri's honor.

The party was supposedly segregated, as well as chaperoned. Turned out it was neither.

Neither, Keira repeated silently, wearily, unable to escape the shadows and shame of the poor decision she had made.

She'd never talked about it. Who would she tell? Her liberal intellectual mother? Her orthodox political father?

There had been no one to talk to, no one to turn to for comfort or advice. And she'd done the only thing she could—she'd moved forward, moved on, moved emotionally and physically, leaving Baraka never to return, eventually leaving England to begin university studies in the States.

A knock sounded at the locked bedroom door. Keira opened the door. A housemaid stood in the hall, holding a garment bag and assorted shopping bags from several of London's most exclusive jewelry boutiques.

"From His Excellency," the maid said, dropping a small curtsey.

A curtsey. For her. Keira would have laughed if she weren't so tired.

"Would you like me to unpack for you, miss?" The house maid offered, carrying the shopping bags into the room.

"No, thank you. I can manage," Keira answered with an uneasy glance at the collection of expensive shopping bags weighting down the maid's arms. It looked as if a fortune had been spent in less than an hour...

"What are those for?" she asked as the maid hung the garment bag in the closet and then placed the remaining bags on the bed.

"You, miss. His Excellency made calls and then sent the driver around to the shops to collect the items."

"I don't understand."

"They're gifts, miss. Presents. His Excellency

does this for all his women." The maid smiled cheerfully. "You're very lucky, aren't you?"

Keira's mouth opened and closed without making a sound. Lucky? Is that what she was?

She half turned, gazed at the handsome bedroom before looking at the maid. "Does he have many women?"

The maid suddenly flushed bright red. "Forgive me, miss. I meant nothing—"

"It's fine." Keira gestured reassurance. "Thank you."

The housemaid moved to the door. "If you need anything, just ring. You've only to ask."

"And Sheikh Nuri? Is he still here…?"

"No, miss, he's gone for the day. But he will be back for dinner."

"I see."

"Dinner will be served at seven. His Excellency dresses for dinner."

"How nice," Keira drawled, more than a little irritated. Kalen had uprooted her, dumped her at his London house, headed off for work or wherever it is he'd gone and was already leaving messages with the maid.

The girl bobbed her head and slipped out the door, closing it quietly behind her.

Keira went to the closet, looked at the garment bag hanging on the rod and then carefully closed the closet door. Just as carefully she moved the shopping bags from her bed.

She wasn't his woman. She didn't want his gifts.

At six-thirty Keira bathed and dressed for dinner. Wrapped in a lettuce-green bath towel, Keira thumbed through her own clothes she'd unpacked earlier and hung in the closet. She'd brought a mishmash of colors and styles and certainly nothing that could be viewed as elegant.

Good.

She'd dress for dinner. She'd just dress like an American woman. Independent. Successful. And free.

Sliding into a pair of old Levi's jeans, Keira drew on a gray pin-striped blouse, the starchy blouse normally worn to work with a conservative suit, but now she let the tail of the shirt hang out, left the collar unbuttoned and twisted her long hair into a half-hazard knot at the back of her head.

No jewelry.

A bit of makeup.

Flat leather loafers.

And she was good to go.

Keira appeared in the dining room at seven on the dot. Kalen was already there, and the maid was right. He had dressed for dinner. Kalen wore black trousers, a black dinner jacket and a white dress shirt which highlighted his golden complexion, his thick black hair, and the amber of his eyes.

Handsome, she thought, drinking him in. He was by far the most handsome man she'd ever met and living in Texas, working for an international company, she'd met a lot of good-looking men.

"You look…" and Sheikh Nuri's voice drifted off as his gaze swept her "…lovely."

She flushed, assailed by guilt. He'd made an effort where clearly she'd made none.

But had she asked to come to London? Had she asked for any of this?

"Thank you," she answered, smiling serenely, successfully hiding her self-doubts. Over the years she'd become very, very good at hiding everything real and true. Self-preservation, she thought, allowing Kalen to seat her at the table.

"Blue's a good color for you," he commented, taking a seat opposite her.

"I'm not wearing blue," she said, glancing down at the thin gray stripes of her blouse. And then she saw her jeans and she understood. "Ah, the Levi's."

"Very chic."

"You did tell the maid to have me dress casually, didn't you?"

His dark eyebrows arched, a challenging light lit his amber eyes. "Is that what she told you?"

"I'm not sure. I didn't understand anything after the His-Excellency-Has-Gone-Out-You-Must-Wait-Here bit."

Kalen's forehead furrowed. "I have a job, *laeela*. Things to do."

"And I have a job, too. I should be in Dallas working, doing what I need to do, not sitting in a bedroom of your house waiting for you to come home!"

"Things have changed. You must adjust."

She had to adjust? Why was she the one who always had to compromise? Sacrifice? Why was she the one who had to give, adjust, change? "I don't want to adjust. I liked my life. I liked my work—"

"Being a cheerleader?"

"You know I worked for Sanford Gas. You know I had a responsible position and I was good." She sat stiffly at the table, temper so hot she thought she might explode. "Too good to just give it all up because you said so."

"So what did you do this afternoon?" he asked, leaning forward to fill their wineglasses.

"Nothing."

"It doesn't have to be nothing. You can rent movies on satellite, watch TV, chat with friends—"

"That's empty activity. I need more."

"Then improve your brain. Read. I have an

extensive library here, and you're free to order books off the Internet."

"Reading is what I do at night before bed. It's not what I do all day." Keira's frustration grew. "Sheikh Nuri, I didn't go to college to play a pampered princess."

"You're angry that I haven't paid you more attention."

She laughed out loud even as she blushed. "I don't even know you! The idea that I could need you—depend on you—is amusing, but untrue."

"You speak boldly for a twenty-three-year-old girl."

"Woman." Her body crackled with tension and it was all she could do to keep her seat. "I'm a woman, and I've grown up with men like you, Sheikh Nuri. Unlike the models and actresses you meet, I don't need your wealth, your notoriety, or your connections."

"My mistress has a sharp tongue tonight."

Her face flamed hotter, her fingers curled around the edge of her chair seat. "I'm not really your mistress. We both know that."

Kalen's eyebrows furrowed. He shot a curious glance around the elegant dining room fragrant with the centerpiece of white orchids and lilies. "Am I missing something, *laeela?* Are you not here, in my home? Are you not taken care of—every need and wish accommodated? Have I not offered you my complete protection?"

She went hot and cold, his word, the endearment *laeela,* once again burning her from the inside out. *Laeela* was such an intimate endearment from a Barakan man and Kalen wasn't the sort of man to flirt lightly. He was serious.

Sheikh Nuri lazily watched Keira who sat tall and rigid across the table from him. Her long dark hair had been pinned back and her cheeks, so ashen last night, glowed hot-pink now.

A high-strung filly, he thought, she was young, sensitive, nervous.

He took a sip from his wine goblet, the robust red filling his mouth, warming his taste buds.

Keira merely fidgeted with her wine. She'd barely touched it.

He should touch her.

He studied her flushed face. Last night she'd been pale like porcelain, a creamy alabaster, but tonight she burned. She glowed. Her dark blue eyes shone, her cheeks flushed a hot feverish pink.

She needed a firm hand. She could use a calming hand.

How convenient. He had two.

"You don't have to be afraid," he said, speaking almost gently, reassuringly. "I will always treat you well."

"I'm not afraid," she answered tersely, and yet when she looked up at him she was all wide blue eyes and apprehension.

No, he thought, she wasn't afraid. She was terrified.

She knew what could happen. She knew just as he did that the tension between them wasn't the usual garden variety of interest. What simmered between them was deep, intense, a heat and interest dating back years…back to when she was just a schoolgirl.

"And you don't have to worry about me," she added, her voice strained, rough. She reached up to push away an inky tendril that had slipped free. "I'm fine."

"*Hamdullah,*" he answered. *Thanks be to God.*

Tears scratched at Keira's throat, the back of her eyes. Until yesterday she hadn't thought she'd ever see him again and yet here she was, a day later, in his home, in his care. It was incredible, impossible, unfathomable. Just looking at him made everything collide and explode inside her, emotions hot and sharp like New Year's fireworks.

Hamdullah. The word echoed in her head and she hurt. No one else made her feel so tense, so nervous, so desperate for more. No one else made her want to throw herself into a river of ice water. No one else…

Hamdullah.

"And you?" she asked formally, continuing the ritual greetings. "How are you?"

"Very well, Miss al-Issidri. Thank you."

"But it's Gordon, Sheikh Nuri, not al-Issidri. I've never used my father's name."

"You did until you were seven."

"How did you know that?"

"I know things that would surprise even you."

She regarded him warily. His eyes were gold, so gold, warmer than she remembered. There was so much about him familiar and even more that wasn't. Was it age? Time? Experience?

Again she glanced at him, a surreptitious glance beneath heavy lashes, seeing again the broad forehead, his long, strong nose, the very square chin which had fascinated her endlessly as a teenager.

Was it possible she'd fallen in love with an image—a face—and not the man?

"Breathe," he said, his gaze never leaving her face.

"I am." But her voice came out too high and thin and she couldn't look at him anymore.

He leaned across the table, an arm extending toward her, his right hand up, palm open. "Give me your hand."

She looked at his hand, the broad palm, the skin lighter than the back of his hand, deep lines etched into the skin and she flashed back to last night, the way he'd touched her on her front porch. Kalen's touch had been like an electrical storm. So hot and bright and fierce. He'd made her feel. And she'd felt absolutely everything.

"Your hand," he repeated softly, commandingly.

She gave her head a half-shake. "Never."

Her gaze slowly traveled up, from the crisp white collar of his shirt, over his bronze columned throat, past his full firm lips to his eyes which looked at her with mockery, challenge, even disdain. Pointedly she held his gaze. "You're not safe."

For a split second he remained expressionless and then his lips curved. His eyes creased. "That just might be the most intelligent thing I've heard you say."

CHAPTER FOUR

"SO WHAT did you think of my gifts?" Kalen asked, lazily switching topics as he leaned forward to top off their wine goblets.

He moved so easily, gracefully, all fluid motion and for a moment she lost concentration, thinking he'd be equally at home on a pony playing polo, astride a camel, pouring mint tea in his desert kasbah.

"Did you like the jewelry?" He added, "I'd hoped you might wear one of the diamond bangles tonight."

Diamond bangles. Weren't the two words incongruous? "I actually didn't open any of the shopping bags."

"No?"

"I don't need, or wear, expensive jewelry."

His lashes dropped over his eyes. "You like cheap jewelry?"

"If I want jewelry, I buy my own."

"You're rejecting my gifts?"

She heard his tone harden, his voice suddenly

reminding her of crushed velvet over steel. "I am not a woman that accepts gifts from strangers—"

"Be careful, *laeela,* before you insult me."

His tone had dropped even lower, husky like whiskey, and she felt a light finger trail her spine, sweeping nerves awake. "I've no desire to insult you, Sheikh Nuri—"

"Kalen. It's Kalen. After all, you want something, remember?"

Heat surged to her cheeks and she sat tall, hands clasped tightly in her lap. "The sooner I return to Texas, the better."

"Return?"

His soft inflection conveyed more than words could. She could see them, two warring parties, and she'd just put his back in the corner. "We've made a point. Shown my father that he can't control me—"

"Your father remains a threat."

"To whom? You? Or me? Because I think you're not worried about me."

"Sidi Abizhaid would never tolerate this kind of frank talk, *laeela.* You would never be permitted to be so confrontational. You would never be permitted to speak publicly, either."

A lump swelled in her throat, large, restrictive. "What do you want from me, Kalen? Tell me so I understand."

"You know what I want. I want you here, with me."

"No. There's more to it than that. This has to do with my father, not me, and I need to understand what he has done. Tell me how a man who has spent his life serving the Nuri family can be considered a threat."

"It's not a topic for discussion."

"Why not? Because I'm a woman?"

Kalen didn't contradict her. Instead he gazed at her from across the gleaming walnut table set with the finest of china and crystal, white taper candles flickering in tall silver candelabras. A profusion of white orchids and lilies spilled from a low round centerpiece.

His silence was a torture and she leaned forward, trying to make him understand. "This is my father, my family, you call a threat. I have every right to know."

"You should spend more time eating and less time arguing."

She shook her head, livid. "You are as bad as them, Kalen. No, make that worse. You don't live in Baraka, you live in England, and you do not dress in robes and head cloths but in Italian suits, but beneath the suit and fine shirts you are just as restrictive, just as rigid and condescending."

He said nothing, his expression blank and she

drew a quick, short breath. "I want to go home, Kalen." She hated feeling so vulnerable, had worked hard to protect herself from feeling this way. Vulnerable was the one thing she couldn't be. Years ago she'd sworn she'd never let anyone hurt her again.

And still he studied her, coolly, dispassionately. He wasn't moved, she thought. He felt nothing. And daggers of pain cut into her heart. "Kalen, hear me. I need to go home. I need my life back." She'd worked so hard to protect herself from this lost feeling, the sense of confusion that came from being torn between parents, homes, cultures, identities. "My life was good for me."

He shifted in his chair, leaning forward, arms folding on the table edge. "Your new life here will be good, too."

"No."

"It is a change, yes, but it will also be good."

"But this isn't my life! This is yours—"

"And yours. Now." He studied her a long moment and when he spoke next, his tone was gentle. "You need to accept that your life has changed. Everything has changed. Permanently."

Accept that overnight she'd been forced from her home, into this odd world where she belonged to a man she knew only from her childhood? It was ridiculous. Preposterous. She wasn't a medieval bride.

"No." Hands shaking, legs feeling like brittle strands of ice, Keira pushed away from the table. "No. You're wrong." Her body was cold and yet her eyes burned hot, gritty, and she blinked, refusing to let one tear form or fall. "You're wrong, Kalen Nuri, about everything."

In her bedroom Keira curled up in one of the overstuffed armchairs and buried her face in the crook of her arm. She wasn't staying here. She couldn't stay here. What was she supposed to *do* here?

The panic rose, filling her, and her eyes felt as if they were dusted with sand but she couldn't cry.

What had happened in Baraka to create such friction between Kalen and her father? And what made Ahmed Abizhaid so dangerous that Kalen refused to see her family and Ahmed's join in marriage?

And was her father really the problem or could the problem be Kalen himself?

She knew her father had never liked the youngest Nuri prince. And yet because of his loyalty to the Sultan, her father had never, could never, voice his suspicion aloud, but from the reports she'd once found on her father's desk she knew her father kept Kalen Nuri under surveillance.

This was more than personal, she thought.

This was bigger than that. So what was it really about?

She needed to know more, needed information. But obviously Kalen wasn't going to tell her anything at this point. So how did she find out what she wanted to know?

Did she go to her father, ask him? Or did she try to get Kalen's trust? Try to get him to open up a little, maybe confide in her?

As if that would ever happen. Sighing, she rubbed her forehead, considered changing for bed but couldn't seem to make herself move. Life had certainly taken an interesting turn...for the worse.

As she sat cross-legged in the armchair, a knock sounded on her bedroom door.

Keira glanced at the clock beside her bed. She'd been in her room for nearly twenty minutes. "Yes?" she called without moving from the chair.

"Open the door."

It was Kalen. Of course. No one else would tell her to open the door. She glared at the door. "I'm sleeping," she said, hunching deeper into the overstuffed armchair.

"You've only been in your room fifteen minutes."

"Twenty."

"Open the door."

"I'm in bed."

"I don't care."

Her jaw dropped, eyes widening. The man was arrogant. "Good night, Kalen."

"Open the door, Keira."

He'd used her given name for the first time. Not Keira Gordon, not Keira al-Issidri. Just Keira. Her skin prickled. Heat lapped at her, more heat in her belly. She drew a breath, and then another, trying to steady her nerves. "I'll see you in the morning." Her voice quavered. "Good night."

"I'm not going anywhere."

She pulled her legs closer to her chest, arms wrapping around her knees, crushing the denim fabric of her jeans. "Then you'll be standing there a very long time."

"Open the door."

"No."

"Keira."

"You can't intimidate me."

She heard him shift outside her door, felt his strength as if it were seeping through the keyhole, sliding beneath the door itself. "This is my house." His voice had dropped.

Goose bumps peppered her flesh. "This is my room."

"So unlock the door for me."

She'd begun to shake. Her grip around her knees felt increasingly weak. "No."

"Why not?" For a moment he sounded almost reasonable.

"Because I'm tired. I have to sleep."

"I heard you had a two-hour nap this afternoon. You can't be that tired." He was still being reasonable. "And since it's not even nine yet, I think you're scared, not tired."

"Go away!"

"And you're not even in bed. You're somewhere by the fireplace. Probably sitting in one of those old club chairs."

Her eyes closed. She exhaled unsteadily. "It's really none of your business, but I am in bed—"

There was a soft scrape and then the sound of the doorknob turning. Keira bolted upright as the door swung open.

"Little fibber," Kalen said, appearing in the doorway.

"You've no right—"

"My house," he interrupted softly, entering her room, narrowed gaze sweeping the perfectly made up bed, the curtains not yet drawn at the windows and all the lamps and overhead lights gleaming brightly. "My woman."

She would have made herself disappear if she could. "I am not your woman."

"You accepted my protection."

"Yes, but that was…" Her voice drifted off and

she gave her head a faint shake. He didn't understand. He didn't want to understand, either.

She saw the hardness in his jaw, the raw male pride in his eyes. He dressed elegantly, clothes covering him in tailored perfection, and yet the exquisite fabric and fine tailoring couldn't cloak the primitive danger of the desert. The desert was about life. Death. Survival.

And she saw the desert in his eyes, dark gold like the Saharan sand. In his bronzed skin, like the copper filigree in the palace ornamentation. In the onyx of his short glossy hair, the same obsidian used to stud the handles of ancient swords.

He was beautiful, but he was what he was. A man.

"So what was it then?" he insisted. "What did you mean when you asked for my help?"

Oh, he was Barakan. All male. And definitely a man of her father's complex world. "I was trapped."

One of Kalen's black eyebrows lifted.

"Trapped," she repeated. "I panicked. I needed help."

"And I gave you help."

"Which I'm grateful for—"

"Which you're not grateful for." He walked toward her, moved slowly, leisurely, a man with

time, money, and power on his side. "You've been
far from grateful."

Any moment he'd have her cornered in her snug
armchair. Any moment and he'd be standing over
her, dominating her yet again. Keira jumped up,
slid over the arm of the chair, before she had no
means of escape. "If you were a gentleman you
wouldn't insist on gratitude. If you were a gentleman you'd need no reward."

His lips curved as she made a hasty retreat across
the room, taking a position by the elegant bed with
the green headboard. "But I want a reward. And
I've no desire to be a gentleman. I leave chivalry
for the French and English."

Her pulse quickened as she saw him turn, face
her, hands on his hips. He wasn't moving but she
felt him approach, felt his strength, his energy,
his force of will. "What is it you want from me
then?"

"To finish what we began."

Her mouth dried. Her heart beat so fast it felt like
lightning streaking in her veins. "I didn't know we
began anything."

"Not so." His jaw flexed, a shadow of a beard
darkening the gold of his skin. "Something was
begun all those years ago when you, sweet shy
schoolgirl, looked at me. You don't think I noticed?
How could I not? Because you, *laeela,* looked at

me with so much hope and curiosity. You looked at me with absolute wonder." His mouth pulled and his smile was downright cruel. "You still do."

She stared at him appalled. Not as much at him, but at herself.

He'd noticed her. He'd known her interest. He knew it now.

She wanted to say something brave and defiant, something tough, flinty, maybe even vulgar but she'd been so infatuated for so long that she simply smiled as her eyes burned.

He was right. He'd been everything wonderful, everything magical, he'd been beautiful and impossible, sexual and sensual and she'd loved the idea that he wasn't all good, that he might have experience, that he willingly flaunted rules.

It had been so appealing somehow. Why?

Kalen took her silence as acquiescence. "You'll want to inform your supervisors at your day job that you won't be returning anytime soon, and you certainly won't be returning to the cheerleading again."

She didn't know what hurt worse—the loss of control, the loss of her lifestyle, or the fact that he'd seen through her all those years ago. "You don't like the cheerleading, do you?"

"No."

"Why not?"

"It's not appropriate."

"For what?" Sarcasm sharpened her tone. "A Barakan woman?"

"For my mistress."

She swallowed hard, words failing her. She'd wondered how he'd envisioned their relationship, wondered how this would work. What exactly did protection encompass? And now she knew. "Men don't have mistresses anymore."

He sounded intrigued. "No?"

She put one hand to her middle, fingers covering the thin cotton blouse as she suppressed the flutter of nerves in her stomach. "And even if they did, I couldn't be your mistress."

"Why not?"

"It's...it would be..." She felt a funny fizz replace the flutter. "Nonsensical."

"Nonsensical?"

"Implausible."

"Implausible?"

Frustration grew. She took a short breath. "Impractical."

Kalen snorted. "Of all your arguments, that is by far your weakest."

Heat washed through her. "How so?"

"Being my mistress would be the most practical solution. It would send an immediate message out, convey in the fewest number of words that you're truly mine, that you belong with me. Live with me." His lips twisted. "Answer to me."

"I answer to no man."

"No man?"

"No one."

His lips pursed, his expression challenging. "You might just be surprised how much you enjoy answering to me."

"Never."

"You want me."

"No."

"I want you." His gaze held hers, long, private, exquisitely intimate. "Very much."

Panic filled her veins, flooded her limbs. "I can't live like this. I won't live like this."

"You'd rather be married to Sidi Abizhaid? You'd enjoy his attentions more?"

"There must be a third option."

"Unfortunately as Omar al-Issidri's daughter there are just two. Your father's choice for you. Or what I offer for you."

"What you offer is degrading. Demeaning."

"Far less demeaning than lying beneath a hairy old Barakan twenty years your senior with visions of civil war in his head." Kalen headed for the door, stopping for a moment as he reached for the brass doorknob. "I would, *laeela,* at least give you pleasure."

She could only stare at him, staggered, over-whelmed by all that he said, all that he'd implied. He was so intense, so…much. He left her no famil-iar landmarks, no guideposts with which to find herself. Center herself.

"Pleasure is no small thing," he added, pulling the door closed. "Sleep well. Good night."

Sleep well? How? How was she supposed to sleep now?

Keira paced and then sat in the middle of her bed, surrounded by a sea of pillows. Eventually she tried to sleep, but couldn't, and then she was pacing again.

What was true, she thought? What was real?

She felt so much at the moment, and yet the emo-tions were so contradictory.

She hated Kalen for doing this, forcing this change, this new life on her, and yet of all the men she'd met in her life, he was the one she wanted most. He was the one man she dreamed of, the one man she craved.

Desire.

Was it mental or physical? Where did desire begin? Where did it end?

What was desire anyway?

She fell asleep—finally—around midnight and the next morning Keira woke early, but discov-ered when she headed downstairs for coffee that

Kalen had been up even earlier. "He's already at his office," the maid said, leading Keira to the breakfast room. "He always goes in early and then returns."

"When he has ladies visit?"

"Yes, miss."

The maid didn't know the meaning of discretion, Keira thought, taking a seat at the breakfast table.

"A newspaper, miss?" The maid offered, extending a stack of international newspapers in Keira's direction.

Keira was delighted by the variety of newspapers, papers from New York, San Francisco, London, Berlin, even a paper from her native Baraka.

Reaching for the Baraka paper, Keira moved her coffee aside and spread the paper out.

It had been years since she followed current events in Baraka, deliberately avoiding news whether it was political or national. She didn't want to think about Baraka or be associated with a culture that made her feel unwanted, undesirable.

The only time she hadn't been able to ignore the news coming from Baraka was when the Sultan, Malik Nuri, married Princess Ducasse several years ago. The media had gone absolutely wild. How could she ignore the wedding when every paper, every television station, even the Internet covered it in breathless detail?

She'd been cynical about Malik's marriage to Princess Nicolette. After all, Nicolette was the most adventurous of the Ducasse princesses, thoroughly Western, highly educated, and yet she'd given up her independence and her glamorous life in the West to marry a sultan.

Cynical, but also envious.

She'd once fantasized about life with Kalen. She'd once wanted to be the one to throw caution to the wind and discover what life would be like with a sheikh, younger brother to the Sultan.

"You look very serious this morning."

Keira jumped at the sound of Kalen's voice and quickly began closing the paper, folding it back the way she'd found it.

"Don't stop reading. It's refreshing to see a woman interested in world events." He moved behind her chair and bending over, dropped a kiss on her brow.

She stiffened in silent protest and yet the moment his lips touched her skin she felt only fire streaking through her, fire and pleasure.

"Next time your lips," he said, taking a seat next to her at the glass topped table.

She scooted her chair back, swung her legs to the other side of her chair, trying to escape his close proximity. "Most women are interested in world events."

"Are they?"

"Yes, they are, which leads me to wonder what kind of women you normally entertain here."

His eyebrows lifted. "Jealous?"

"Merely curious."

"Interesting." He leaned back as the maid placed his coffee on the table in front of him. "Have you had breakfast yet, or are you waiting for me?"

"I didn't wait."

"Good. I wouldn't want you ever famished, or thirsty." His eyes gleamed. "Just hungry for me."

Keira's temper spiked and she forced herself to take a breath, relax. "Why do you do this? The innuendos? Suggestive comments? The constant sexual commentary?"

"But this is what you wanted." He took a sip from his cup, lashes lowered, concealing his expression. "This is what you've always wanted from me."

"Wrong."

"This is who I am."

But she didn't believe it. Kalen might be a rebel, but he was also an intellectual. She knew he'd left Baraka because he'd wanted more out of life. "I don't agree."

"*Laeela,* you don't even know me."

"But I used to watch you." The admission slipped

out before she could think better of it. She flushed, her cheeks now nearly as warm as the rest of her. "You weren't this provocative with others. You were more...sincere."

Abruptly he leaned forward, leaning so close she could see each and every gold fleck in his eyes, the dense black lashes surrounding his eyes, the warm bronze texture of his skin. "So why am I behaving like this with you?"

He was beautiful, she thought, too beautiful, indecently beautiful for a man. Rugged jaw, hard, almost harsh cheekbones, and then softened just enough by that mouth, and suddenly she couldn't think, couldn't remember her argument or why she was even arguing with him in the first place.

"Why?" he repeated.

But no words, no explanation came. She was gone. Lost. Sixteen again and her belly in knots, her nerves dancing everywhere, curious, aware.

A kiss, one kiss, his hands closing around her shoulders, bringing her near, bringing her into his circle of warmth.

"You were saying?" he encouraged. "You've got me hanging on every word, *laeela*."

If only it were true, she thought distractedly, fascinated by his mouth, briefly undone by the fullness of his lower lip, the way the upper lip curved. It was a firm mouth, wide, mobile. His mouth on her neck, his mouth on her collarbone, the curve of her breast.

"You're trying to prove a point," she said at last, forcing the words out even as she forced air back into her lungs. For a split second time had stopped. For a moment there had only been space and emotion, hope and sensation. Timelessness. The fall of boundaries.

Bliss.

He half smiled and yet the intensity in his eyes burned her, all the way through. "And what would my point be, Keira?"

It required an effort to think. She was still trying to ground herself, shove her spirit inside her skin. "I suppose, that you're in charge."

"You suppose?"

"To let me know you're in control."

"But I am in control," he answered mildly, and yet the mildness was deceptive. She felt the authority behind his words, the absolute power in his body.

"Which is exactly what I don't want."

"Why?"

"Because you shouldn't be in control of me. I should be in control, at least of me and my world."

"Maybe you should trust me."

"Trust what? Trust how? We're so different." She

reached for an orange from the fruit bowl on the table and dug her thumbnail into the shiny peel, impatiently tugging back the first scrap of skin. "Too different."

He reached over, took the orange from her and with a small knife finished peeling it for her. Splitting the orange open he divided a section and put the segment to her lips. "Men and women usually are."

The orange section felt cool and slick against her lips and yet she couldn't open her mouth, couldn't take the fruit into her mouth when he was watching her so closely.

"Take it," he said.

Her throat sealed closed. "I can—"

And as she opened her mouth to refuse, he slid the fruit in, against her tongue and teeth. She bit down, lips instinctively closing, juice spurting tart and sweet. Her cheeks grew hot beneath his intense gaze. She could barely chew and swallow, conscious of the fullness of her cheeks and the trickle of juice running from the corner of her lips.

Abruptly he leaned forward, kissed the edge of her mouth, his tongue lapping at the juice on her lips before sliding across the seam of her lips.

Everything inside her felt hot, explosive, her belly clenching and unclenching as desire rushed through her hot, wanton, provoked.

His kiss, that sudden sexy kiss, made her want and made her thighs press and she knew he was far more dangerous to her safety—and sanity—than anything her father had planned for her. "You scare me," she choked, pulling away.

He merely smiled, lazily, indulgently, a virile man in complete control. "You scare yourself." He pulled another section of orange apart.

Hot, tense, Keira didn't think she'd ever been so aware of anyone before. She stared at his hands, at the way he cupped the peeled orange, the fruit so small and veined white against the darker gold of his skin. She watched his long fingers bend around the fruit, his nails short, filed neatly, and then he was holding another section out to her.

She viewed the orange section suspiciously. "Why would I scare myself?"

"Because you want to feel calm. Peaceful. But physical desire isn't peaceful."

"I'm not talking about desire."

"Actually, you are."

Keira reached for the orange quickly, before she lost courage and yet the moment her fingers brushed his she saw the gleam in his golden gaze.

"But you're afraid of what you feel," he added, his black lashes lowering but not concealing his open interest. "Afraid of the attraction."

"I'm not afraid of you."

"Just afraid of what I'd do to you if we were alone and my hands were on you."

Keira crushed the orange between her fingers, the fruit never making it to her lips. Sticky juice ran between her fingers, staining her palm. "You'd do nothing."

"I'd do everything."

She ducked her head, blood rushing through her in a dizzying sweep of heat. He was right. She wanted. But she feared desire, particularly her desire for him. If she wanted experience there had to be a better way…if she wanted sex she should find someone less complex, less demanding because Kalen was demanding in every way. "Please, Sheikh Nuri—"

"Please, Kalen."

Her blush deepened, her face burning from hairline to chin, even her mouth feeling soft, swollen, sensitive. "You mustn't say things like that. Kalen."

"Why not? Keira."

She looked at him helplessly, seeing what she'd always seen—ruthless beauty, sensuality, a hint of savagery, and her belly knotted, and knotted again, making her aware of the emptiness inside her.

He had to know what he was doing to her, had to know she could hardly sit still, her womb hot, heavy, her breasts just as full. A body taut with need.

A life of unanswered want.

She'd risked everything to see him that night at the party, risked her father's wrath, the shame that would come from attending a party for adults not teenage girls. She hadn't cared. She'd only wanted to see him, be near him, and in risking everything that night, she'd lost everything, too.

Innocence. Dignity. Self-esteem.

Stripped from her by a drunk cruel male, neither a boy nor a man, just a male that wanted something she'd never given to anyone.

Kalen suddenly caught the back of her head in his palm and held her face still, forcing her to be quiet for him. Once she was caught, held motionless by his touch, the desire blazing in his eyes, he lowered his head and his lips brushed across her lips, brushed the curve of her cheekbone, and then he placed the lightest, most excruciating kiss on the side of her neck. She shivered as his lips burned her skin, shivered as his lips repeated the kiss and fire licked her from the inside out.

She wanted. She wanted him.

But if he knew the truth about her, he'd lose all desire for her, as well as respect.

Finally Kalen's head lifted and he half smiled down into her eyes. "I will have you," he said quietly, and his smile had nothing to do with amusement and everything to do with control. "I will hold you. It's just a matter of time."

CHAPTER FIVE

HE WAS right, she thought, heart racing, palms damp. The way things were going it would just be a matter of time before he possessed her.

It seemed inevitable the way things were going. The way she was responding.

She wasn't just losing control. She'd lost control. Everything about him had a dizzying effect, a weakening of her defenses. He made the logical, rational part of her disappear leaving just the woman hungry for touch.

Hungry for him.

If only she could isolate the thing which affected her so, but it wasn't one thing, it was everything. The way he looked. The way he smelled. The way he touched her. Kissed her.

Keira drew an unsteady breath, head still spinning, body too warm. She'd only been here with him twenty-four hours and already he'd reduced her to dumb need and desperate skin.

She couldn't stay here, in his house, in his world.

She couldn't let this seduction of the mind and senses continue.

Kalen regarded her quizzically. "You look pale," he said.

"I could use some air," she admitted. A lot of air. And maybe one long cold shower. How could she feel like this? How could she respond like this? She'd thought she was cold, frigid, hopelessly repressed and yet something about Kalen made touch seem so natural, skin a pleasure and a comfort.

"Then let's get out, go for a walk, do some errands. We could both use a diversion, I think."

Fifteen minutes later, in the back of the limousine, as the leafy green of Kensington parks and gardens gave way to thick city traffic, Keira felt the first whisper of reality return.

What on earth was she doing with Kalen Nuri, she wondered, watching him make a series of quick phone calls. Kalen Nuri. Sheikh Kalen Nuri. A man easily ten years her senior and a hundred years older in terms of experience and expectations.

How could she be sitting here with him, a purse on her arm, high heels on her feet, cocooned in the back of his limo as if this was routine? This wasn't routine and she wasn't thinking. She'd turned her brain off but she had to wake up now. Sheikh Kalen Nuri wasn't Prince Charming. He was the problem sheikh. The rebel. The Nuri renegade.

"You don't know how to relax," Kalen said, glancing at her between calls.

"I am relaxed."

His lips twisted. "As relaxed as a big caged cat."

"You spend a lot of time with big cats then?"

One black eyebrow lifted and he slid his phone back into his jacket pocket. "Your father doesn't know the first thing about you, does he?"

"What does that mean?"

"You are nothing like a traditional Barakan woman, and your groom wants a traditional wife. Do you know your groom?"

"He's not my groom—"

"Just your fiancé."

"He's not my fiancé, either. I never agreed to marry Mr. Abizhaid."

"You don't have to agree. Not if your father promises your hand."

She said nothing, knowing Kalen was right. In Baraka her father could marry her against her wishes. It was an archaic law, one the Sultan had been working on changing, but so far hadn't been accepted by the people.

"Your father doesn't know you're a cheerleader, either, does he?" Kalen persisted.

Of course her father didn't know. If her father

knew he would have locked her up years ago. "No."

"If your fiancé finds out, he'll have your father's head."

Unease whispered through her. She curled her fingers into her palms. "Hopefully he won't find out."

"Hopefully."

His echo heightened her own internal struggle. "I didn't ask for this conflict," she said, knowing that her father was orthodox, conservative, right-wing—and what was she supposed to do? Divorce her family? Adopt a new culture? She was who she was, and even if she changed her name, she couldn't change her ethnicity.

"But you had to know that becoming a professional cheerleader for an American football team would shame your father?"

"Me becoming a cheerleader had nothing to do with my father. I dance because I was trained as a dancer. It's something I enjoy, and if I was defying someone, it wasn't my father." She took a quick breath. "It was my mother. My liberal, feminist, activist mother. Happy?"

His brow furrowed. "No."

She lifted a hand in weary surrender. "I spent my entire life pulled between my parents, dragged between two homes. I'm neither English, nor Barakan.

In my mother's eyes, I was never smart enough. In my father's eyes I'm too educated. Quite frankly, there are times I don't know who I am or what I'm supposed to be."

"So you go to America and become a Dallas Cowboy cheerleader?"

"Why not? They accepted me. They liked me. They weren't always fixating on what I was doing wrong." Glancing out the window she noticed that they were nearing New Bond Street, expensive shops, designer fashions, and yet she felt exhausted, already worn-out. "I'd rather go to America and be my own invention than remain in Baraka or England and be nothing."

"You've never been nothing. Many men have wanted you, *laeela*. It's you that hasn't wanted them."

Her upper lip curled in disgust. "Is being wanted by a man supposed to validate me somehow? Make me feel like a woman?"

"Doesn't it?"

"No!" Her hands fisted. "No. I don't need a man to be interesting, or important, or complete. I am fine just the way I am, thank you very much."

Kalen stunned her by suddenly clapping. And it wasn't just a short, single clap, but a slow, firm applauding that made her jaw drop.

He was applauding *her*.

"That is," he said quietly, his expression hard, his tone decisive, "the second most intelligent thing I've heard you say."

The limousine slowed and parked before a street of gleaming shops. The chauffeur opened the back door, waited while Kalen assisted Keira out.

"Let's window-shop," Kalen said, indicating the row of shops where each window display was more expensive and sophisticated than the last. "Where should we start?"

"I don't care. It's just fun to be out. What are your errands? What do you want to do?"

Kalen stared at her for a long minute, a half smile playing at his lips. "Spoil you."

She frowned. "I don't need anything."

"Maybe not. But you want things."

"No—"

"Yes."

She stared at him incredulously. "Does every woman do what you want?"

"Yes."

Stay calm, she told herself. "I'm not every woman."

"Just my woman."

She shot a just as frustrated glance. "I didn't ask to become your woman. I asked for your protection—"

"Exactly."

"—thinking it would be momentary. A quick lifeline, a toss of a life jacket..."

"You thought wrong."

"Kind of you to point it out."

"I told you, I leave chivalry to the French and English. Now we shop. My way."

Arguments gone, energy depleted, Keira gave in, allowing him to make the purchases he was determined to make. And he was serious about buying, she quickly discovered. Kalen knew exactly where he wanted to go, knew precisely what he was looking for. The salesclerks in the various boutiques knew him, too.

In store after store Kalen pointed to this, to that, ordering one of something, three of another. There were day clothes, evening clothes, coats, shoes, boots, purses, accessories. Keira kept shaking her head, protesting that she didn't need so much, that it was wasteful to buy so much but Kalen ignored her, signing credit card purchase after credit card purchase.

"Tell me we're done," Keira pleaded as the limousine picked up another armload of shopping bags. Her mother had always been so disdainful of fashion, saying that intelligent women needed assertiveness, not artifice, while her father thought women should be robed and shrouded and left in the back of the house.

"Almost."

"What's left to buy? We've shoes, coats, day wear, evening gowns…"

"Your undergarments."

It took her a moment to realize he was talking about taking her shopping for underwear and her legs felt odd, all weak and quivery. *"No."*

"You need lingerie."

"That's personal." She was mortified that they were even having this conversation.

"Men buy lingerie for women all the time."

"Not for me."

His thick black lashes dropped, lifted, his golden gaze curiously possessive. "Until now."

His words hung in the air between them and her stomach flipped inside out. Heat spread through her, heat and the strange awareness that they were tied together in this, and not just now, but forever.

Forever…

She swallowed, fought for calm. "Let me at least buy my own underwear." Her voice came out husky, almost sexual and she looked away, confused by the dual nature of desire—attraction and fear. Did all women feel this way when confronted by a man innately sensual…overwhelmingly sexual?

"Sorry. Can't. You'd be running off to the nearest cheap department store first thing."

She grasped at the hint of normal conversation. "And what's wrong with that?"

"Nothing. If you're a nice middle-class English woman." His gaze found hers, held, challenging her. "And you're no nice, middle-class English woman."

Fascinated, she let him hold her gaze, let him look at her as though he owned her and fire prickled across the tops of her cheekbones, through the inside of her lower lips, across her rib cage into the tips of her breasts. "What am I then?"

"You know what you are."

"But you've made no claim..." Her voice faded, her courage failing. "I mean merely that there's nothing legal, or contractual..."

"You think paperwork will change a thing?" His upper lip curled, hinting at what lay behind his veneer of civilization, hinting at the real man—the primal, savage male. "You think I'd let anyone take you from me now?"

She couldn't speak.

He laughed, so low, so roughly that she felt as if he'd taken her clothes and peeled them off her just as he'd taken the skin from the small sweet orange this morning at breakfast. "I'd kill the man that touched you."

Shivering inwardly, she nearly put a hand to her throat. "You can't say that."

"I can say whatever I want." His eyes flashed dangerously. "And so can you. You should always speak your mind with me. Even if I don't agree."

She felt her eyes widen and she gave her head a faint vague shake. "You're Barakan."

"Yes."

"A sheikh."

"Yes."

And then she could think of nothing else to say. But maybe that was enough. Maybe that was all she needed to say.

"Let's finish our shopping so we can head home and relax," he said, placing a hand in the small of her back, steering her toward the next boutique, his palm touching the curve of her spine, his hand felt hot, her body alive and very sensitive.

Suddenly he was standing close to her, very close and she felt his hips brush her bottom, his shoulders against her back. His head tipped, his mouth touched the shell of her ear. "You'll like beautiful lingerie, *laeela*. You'll like the way I cover you in the sheerest, softest laces, silks and satin. You'll feel a little bit wicked, very bare, and pampered beyond your wildest imagination."

His breath caressed her ear, warm against her heated skin, her body hummed from the nearness of him.

She felt his hand stroke the curve of her hip, over

the roundness of her backside. "I will take care of you, *laeela,* as no man ever has, as no man ever could."

Heady, terrifying words.

Keira swayed, felt his hand tighten more firmly on her hip, the press of fingers against her sensitive pelvic bone, his palm wide, covering more of her skin. "Let me dress you," he whispered in her ear, "so I can undress you. Again and again."

This had to stop. She had to get control back. Had to reassert herself again. Her eyes half-closed, she dragged in air, trying desperately to clear her head. "Stop. Stop whatever it is you're doing to me."

"I'm doing nothing."

"You're doing everything."

He laughed softly, supremely confident, his breath tickling her nape. "*Laeela,* we haven't even begun."

In the lingerie shop Kalen only bought filmy, delicate nightgowns, and lacey, delicate bras and panties, his taste very European, each set costing at least three hundred pounds, some four and five hundred.

Keira was staggered by the amount she saw tallied on the bill. It was more money than she made in a month. Working two jobs. "Kalen, no," she whispered as the bits of silk and lace were wrapped up in heaps of tissue. "It's too extravagant, far, far too much money."

"Yes, Kalen. Darling. Far, far too much money." A husky feminine voice repeated.

Keira looked at Kalen and then at the woman who'd joined them, the woman a stunning blonde, tall, slender and yet blessed with goddesslike proportions.

"Hilary." Kalen wasn't smiling, but he wasn't frowning, either. His expression was perfectly... expressionless.

"Shopping again?" Hilary said, and she was smiling. A wide, hard, bitter smile that didn't touch anything but her lips.

Kalen didn't answer and Hilary smiled even harder, strong white teeth flashing. "If you've got your wallet out, darling, don't forget to buy something for me. I'm sure you remember my size. You used to love dressing me. Remember? Everything silky, satin, everything lace."

Keira's stomach rose. She wanted to be sick. Looking away, she tried to fix on a point beyond the shop window but it was impossible to shut out Kalen's noncommittal answer, or Hilary's seething angry energy.

Keira excused herself, turned to a shopgirl, asked for directions to the ladies' washroom, escaping the tension for the small pink marble lavatory.

In the washroom she washed her hands under icy cold water and drew several deep, but shaky breaths. Hilary, whoever Hilary was, scared the hell out of her. She knew women like Hilary existed, but Keira didn't want to know women like Hilary.

The bathroom door opened, closed and Keira looked up to see Hilary standing there, hands on hips, studying her. Hilary was still smiling, but the bitterness was gone, replaced now by arrogance, smiling the dazzling toothy smile of a woman much photographed, confident in her physical beauty and perfection.

"You're not the first." Hilary moved toward her, a slow catwalk that would have been striking on a fashion show runway but was instead disturbing in the small pink washroom.

"I've no idea what you're talking about," Keira said, calmly rinsing the perfumed soap suds off her hands.

"Come on, it's just us girls now. We can be honest." Hilary leaned against the far edge of the marble counter. "You're the new girl. The new plaything for him to spoil. Been there. Done that."

Keira grabbed for one of the paper towels to dry her hands. "That's not how it is."

"Sure it is. Let's see if I can refresh your memory. Diamond bangles. A new wardrobe. Extravagant lingerie—only the finest silks and laces for him to take on and off." Hilary's green eyes narrowed with the feral intensity of her smile. "Sound familiar?"

Keira's throat sealed closed. She couldn't have answered even if her life depended on it.

"You know what's coming next, don't you?" Hilary continued, arms folding in satisfaction. "You'll be given keys to your new place—the sexy penthouse for the sexy mistress—but you'll know you're in the club when you get your very own scarf. Red. His signature color. All the girls have them."

"All the girls?" Keira echoed faintly, reeling.

"All the girls." Hilary's brows beetled. "As I said, you're not the first. And you won't be the last. The sheikh doesn't keep anyone long."

"You've got it all wrong."

"Or maybe you do. I've known him for three years, been his lover for almost two, and that's a long time for Kalen. He's not a man to be caught, kept, he's not about to give up his lifestyle to make any woman happy."

"And what is his lifestyle?"

"It's whatever he wants it to be…whatever he wants to do. Go on a trip. Take another lover—"

"I'd never put up with it."

"You say that now, but you'll change. You'll

realize there are advantages to being Sheikh Nuri's woman, financial and social advantages to being taken care of by one of the world's most powerful men."

Keira felt trapped. "I'm not interested in power. Or money. I can buy things myself."

"Ah." Hilary's lips curved mysteriously. "Can you pleasure yourself as well, too? Because no one— and I mean no one—knows how to love a woman like Kalen Nuri."

Blood rushed to Keira's cheeks, her body growing dangerously hot, a heat she didn't understand and couldn't explain. All she knew was that she needed out, away, and swiftly she exited the washroom for the now empty shop.

Kalen stood outside the store, next to the waiting limousine. "Everything okay?" he asked, a faint frown marking his brow.

"Yes." She slid into the back of the limo, scooted across the seat and crossed one leg over the other, trying hard to hide the fact that she was trembling.

The scene with Hilary had completely, thoroughly unnerved her.

Undone her.

She could feel Kalen's gaze as the limousine pulled away from the curb but she couldn't look at him, couldn't make eye contact. Hilary had said such awful things and yet she'd also spoken the truth.

Could truth be so ugly?

And it wasn't just the gifts...the mention of the diamond bangles, the lavish shopping trip, but the fact that women craved Kalen's lovemaking...the fact that she, Keira, craved Kalen's lovemaking...

Bad, bad, bad, this was so bad. Keira pressed a knuckled fist to her mouth, pressed back the wave of nausea threatening to overwhelm her. But she wasn't like the women who wanted him for his money or power. All these years she'd loved him for himself...

Love.

She used the word love. But it wasn't love, couldn't be love...

"You spoke with Hilary?" Kalen's voice broke the heavy silence.

Keira looked up. Her lips tugged. "I think it's more accurate to say, she spoke with me."

"What did she say?"

"Oh, the usual stuff and nonsense people like to say about sheikhs."

Kalen's features were hard, a granite mask. He wasn't in a laughing mood. "Which is?"

"I want you for your money. I want the lifestyle."

"Nothing about the great sex?" he asked, deadpan.

Anguish filled her, but she smiled to hide the depth of her emotion. "Sorry. She didn't mention anything about good, much less, great sex." *Lies, lies, lies,* she silently mocked, smiling even wider, feeling even sicker. She'd never felt so lost in her entire life.

"I'm disappointed."

"Of course you would be."

"What does that mean?"

She shot him a look of disbelief. "What do you think?"

He liked it when she looked at him like that. Suspicious. Mistrustful. And yet still so curious.

What was it she wanted when she looked at him with eyes so wide, so deeply blue?

What was it she imagined he could give her?

She was right. She wasn't Barakan, and she wasn't English, either. But she was beautiful, exotic, and he'd lived in the West long enough he couldn't stomach the idea of women being kept apart, didn't want to just sit with men at dinner, didn't want lovely women robed, hidden. Women were like precious art. A beautiful woman made everything more interesting. A beautiful woman should be viewed, revered, respected.

He told people he was too liberal for Baraka, that

he'd become too Western and that's why he'd moved to London. But of course it wasn't the truth.

The truth?

He hadn't left Baraka at all. He might appear to be a man who'd left responsibility and family behind, a man who'd settled comfortably, easily into a decadent lifestyle in London, but his heart lay in Baraka.

His work was there, too.

His business was a cover. And yes, he made money off companies, dealt in the stock market, bought and sold corporations when it suited him and his financial portfolio, but the business deals were a front for his real work.

His real work. Now there was a deeply held secret. He never talked about his real work.

"Why have you never married?" Keira asked, her tone suddenly flinty.

"Not interested," he answered with a shrug. And I don't make long-term commitments."

"Yet you're in your thirties."

"Your point being?"

"You don't want love? Children? Family?"

He looked at her, seeing each and every long black eyelash, the blue of her eyes with flecks of lavender, the full bow shape of her mouth. He could almost imagine her lush beauty when ripe with his child. No one would be more beautiful. No one would be more spirited. "No."

"Never?"

"Never."

He'd silenced her finally. She sank back against the black leather seat, her dark hair a glossy contrast in textures, her blue eyes intense, almost haunting in the sudden pallor of her face.

For a moment he could have sworn he saw a sheen of tears in her eyes, then her smooth jaw firmed, her throat worked and she closed her eyes, inky lashes so dark and dense against pale ivory cheeks. When her eyes opened again, they were dry.

He suddenly felt too harsh, too abrupt. "I've chosen mistresses instead of girlfriends because it's convenient for me," he said by way of explanation, "as it is for them. I'm a rich man. Women love rich men."

"Disgusting," she muttered.

She was livid. She was trying hard to hide the intensity of her emotions and the effort fascinated him.

He resisted the urge to pull her off her seat and onto his, even though he wanted nothing more than to tilt her head back, reveal her neck and tender skin to his mouth, his lips, his tongue.

He wanted her.

Needed her.

His body hardened knowing that her body would fit him, knowing her softness would suit him.

Yet desire required intelligence. Respect. Restraint. Desire required seduction. Desire required satisfaction.

Kalen felt harder than ever. He'd like to lose himself in her and if she weren't so inexperienced, he'd take her now. He'd like to part her legs, settle her on his lap, fill her with him, burying himself deep. He could feel her body tighten around him, feel her shudder in his hands, her hips caught in his hands, her shoulder delicate and sweetly scented against his mouth.

The air had grown thick in the car and Keira dragged in air, finding it increasingly hard to breathe. Something was happening, she thought, feeling as if Kalen had somehow put a match to her skin.

Fire, awareness, tension.

And the tension was growing thicker by the second.

Odd, she thought distractedly, knowing he wasn't even looking at her and yet knowing she was the object of his attention. He wanted her.

She wanted him, could almost feel him despite the physical distance between them.

She could feel his hands settle on her hips, feel his

body rub against hers. His skin would be smooth, taut, incredibly warm.

Eyes half closing she tried to ignore the curl of hunger in her belly, the hunger saying fill me, answer me, sate me.

His thighs parting her thighs. His warm hard body where hers was equally warm but very soft. The slow surrender of giving herself over to him and the senses crying out for release. Relief. Let me go. Let me free.

What it would be like to have him enter her? Love her? Would he be good to her? Generous with her?

She looked at him, unable to hide anything, and when his eyes met hers she could have sworn he knew exactly what she was thinking.

Yes, she thought, the heat continuing to rise, to build, to wash through her little waves on top of other waves, he'd be good. He'd be generous. He'd be what she'd always hoped a man would be.

His fingers curving around her hipbones. His touch strong. Sure. His head bending, his mouth covering her own.

His lips testing, tasting, making her just want him more. Making her want endlessly.

She touched the tip of her tongue to her upper lip, her breathing ragged, her skin hot, flushed, the desire secret and yet not.

"So what do you think?" Kalen asked, gesturing out the window.

What did she think? About what?

Keira felt as if she were swimming up, up through a sea of need and desire and her body felt languid.

It was hard to focus, even harder to speak. "Think about what?" she asked, slowly surfacing and feeling completely spent by the effort.

"Your new home." Kalen was looking out the window. "It's the building ahead of us."

Her brain wasn't working. Just her nerves, her senses, her incredible craving for contact, for Kalen's body, for his hidden skin.

They'd just crossed the Thames and ahead of them was a sleek new building built on the banks of the river. The tall building seemed to be an endless expanse of steel and glass.

Why did she have a new home? Why had she ever left Dallas? Nothing was making sense anymore. Least of all her own desires. "This isn't where you live."

"No. It's where you live." He paused, let his words sink in. "When you're not sleeping with me."

And suddenly Hilary's face, grinning like the Cheshire cat, danced before Keira's eyes. *Just wait until you get the keys to the sexy penthouse suite...*

Keira's chest tightened, emotion so hot it burned.

Everything Hilary had said had been true. The jewelry. The shopping. The exquisite lingerie. And now the penthouse.

Hurt, outraged, Keira felt tears burn behind the back of her eyes but she wouldn't let them fall. She curled her fingers into fists, lifted her chin and kept her gaze fixed on the sleek glass and steel building which soared up, twenty stories into the sky.

If Kalen thought he could just stick her in an apartment and expect her to wait for him, he was wrong.

He might think she was his woman, he might even treat her like his mistress, but that didn't mean she'd agreed to play the part.

Drop me off, she silently vowed. Say goodbye. I don't care. Because as soon as you go, I'm leaving, too.

CHAPTER SIX

HE'D done this many, many times before, she thought, as he introduced her to her new apartment the same way he'd introduced her to her new life.

Kalen was calm, matter-of-fact, opening doors, pointing out closets, luxury items, artwork, knickknacks.

How many other women had he put here in this sumptuous apartment? How many other women had he taken on the tour, showing off the view from the living room, the bedroom, the sunken tub in the bathroom?

She felt icy as he concluded the tour, leading her back to the living room, the room where they started. The apartment had been decorated with that elusive taste only money can buy—antique carved screens from the Far East, fat wood Buddhas, a column of jade-green fish, each identical, stacked on top of each other nine feet high. Sleek Scandinavian inspired chairs squaring off against white linen-covered sofas that stretched beneath the massive plate glass windows overlooking the Thames.

"All this for me," she jested, her voice rising, too high and thin.

He shrugged. "You need your own space when you're not with me."

"So I'm allowed freedom? I can go out on my own?" She sounded as if she were mocking him, but she wanted information. How much independence was he going to give her? If she left, how much time would she have before he found out?

"Of course you can go out, chaperoned, but not on your own. It's not safe."

"Safe? Safe for whom? We're not in Baraka, Kalen."

"No. And nor do you want to be." His expression hardened, turned forbidding. "Trust me on this one, *laeela,* you do not want to go back, not now, not after what's happened to your...reputation."

He'd said the last word delicately, as if there was anything delicate about a ruined reputation. She laughed a little, and felt her legs wobble. "Is my reputation ruined then?"

"Nearly."

"What would it take to destroy it completely?"

"Another week or two alone with me."

Then that wouldn't be a problem. She didn't intend to even stay the night.

"But it's already damaged," Kalen added, as if he could read her thoughts. "Everyone knows what has happened. Everyone in Baraka is talking."

Keira slowly sat down on one of the low silk couches dominating the living room. "How long do you plan on keeping me?" Two weeks, maybe four, she thought he'd say.

But he didn't immediately answer. He seemed lost in thought and then his broad shoulders shifted. "Forever."

"Forever?"

"I've no intention of ever letting you go."

"Hilary said—"

"Hilary's not here."

Keira stared out of one of the enormous windows overlooking the river, her mind blank, mercifully so. She didn't think she could handle a single thought at this point in time, not after everything she'd been through.

Life was interesting.

Sometimes too interesting.

Eventually she forced herself to gather her thoughts, regain her composure. "But you've said you'll never marry, and I never wanted to be anyone's mistress."

"You're not just anyone's mistress. You're mine."

"I don't see the distinction."

He thrust a glass of wine into her hand. "You will."

Keira accepted the white wine gratefully. She'd never needed anything as much as she needed the wine right now.

They'd had a late lunch while shopping earlier, popping into the cozy paneled Polo Lounge at the Westbury Hotel on Bond Street, but since then nothing, and she desperately needed to forget.

Forget him, forget her, forget the situation and all the damaging words.

She'd suspected he was hard, had heard rumors of his ruthlessness, even read a report lying on her father's desk that suggested Kalen Nuri was dangerous—a threat to many that worked in the palace—and yet she hadn't wanted to believe it. She'd wanted him to be good, kind, heroic.

Kalen Tarq Nuri was not heroic.

Pain rushed through her and she half closed her eyes, not knowing what to think, not understanding what she was feeling, either. And yet with eyes closed all she could see was the incredible penthouse apartment with its expensive artwork, the luxurious and eclectic furnishings. The apartment included a butler. A cook. A housekeeper.

For one apartment.

For one woman—whatever woman—Kalen Nuri chose to spoil this week.

She'd been cold and now she felt feverishly hot. Furious that she'd been brought here. Livid that she was the woman of the week.

Keira drew a breath, and then another. Her chest felt as if it were on fire and she pressed the wine to her mouth, trying to cool the fury raging inside. But the anger just grew. How could he do this to her? Especially as he knew how she'd once felt about him. "How long has it been since your last mistress lived here?"

"Hilary never lived here."

"But other women have?"

She saw his jaw flex, saw the flare of temper in his eyes. "The apartment has been empty for months. You haven't chased anyone out."

Keira took another sip of wine. The cold tart wine washed her tongue, slid easily down her throat. "Months without a woman? That's admirable."

Anger tightened his features, thickening his jaw further. "I've had women, *laeela*. I just haven't supported one financially lately."

Tension flared between them hot and fierce and Keira rose from the white linen sofa. She stepped carefully—pointedly—around Kalen and walked to the window.

He was so arrogant. So incredibly ruthless. A sheikh in all his glory. A sheikh reveling in his power.

Bastard.

She swallowed quickly, hating the stupid rush of hurt and anger. She didn't want to feel like this, didn't like feeling like this. Calm was so much better. Detachment infinitely more comfortable. But around Kalen she felt only wild emotion.

This had to stop. She had to get control back. Calm, she reminded herself. Reason. Logic.

Still clutching her wine goblet, she gazed out at the river, the view of Parliament, Big Ben, the Tower Bridge. Once this area of London had been industrial, run-down, far beyond the borders of polite society and now it was developed for the rich, the modern, the trendy.

The fury returned. And this is where Sheikh Nuri installed his mistresses. This is where Kalen intended to keep her. Everything Hilary said had been true.

He was worse than a bastard. He'd break her heart. Again.

Drawing a painful breath, her gaze fell to her wineglass, the sides of the goblet already clouding with condensation. The wine was the palest shade of gold, clear, very clear, reminding her of the sunlight as it washed over the dunes of sand in the early hours of the morning. Sharp. Hard. Bright.

She couldn't let this happen. She had to make

him understand. "I am not like your other women." Her words were barely audible but she knew he heard her. "I do not deserve this. Especially not from you...a fellow countryman. A Barakan."

He said nothing and she turned to look at him. He stood in front of the empty hearth, his broad shoulders dwarfing the natural stone mantel. "You know how important a woman's reputation is, Kalen. You know what you do to me."

"Your father can't be trusted."

"So you destroy me? Ruin my reputation, change my life?"

"You will be compensated."

"How?" She demanded hotly, her eyes growing gritty. She knew she was leaving, but she wanted answers anyway. He owed her answers. He owed her the truth. "With what? Money? Gifts?" The pain was getting worse, the hurt nearly intolerable. "Pleasure in your bed?"

Kalen walked toward her. "You will have all that, and more."

"More?" She laughed to conceal her sudden flurry of nerves. Kalen was nearly in front of her now and she had nowhere to go, nowhere to run. And she needed to run. She needed to run for her very life. "You jest, Your Excellency. You mean less."

"Your Excellency," he repeated, and with two

fingers he touched her brow, tracing one delicately arched eyebrow, fingers sliding from winged brow to her hairline. "You're afraid of me. You needn't be. I'd never hurt you."

She couldn't hide her shudder. One touch and she burned for him. One touch and she wanted to take his hand and press it to her, wanted to experience more pressure, more pleasure, more sensation. "You've hurt me already." Her voice nearly broke. "You've forced me here, compromised my reputation—"

"I'm not all bad, *laeela*. I can be very gentle. And patient. I have trained many falcons, learned to work with the most timid to the most fierce, the wild to the wounded. I shall be as gentle and patient with you. I promise."

She couldn't look away from his face, from the heat in his gold eyes, from the sensual shape of his lips. Her stomach twisted, plummeted. "I do not want you."

"You do. But something stops you, and I do not think it is modesty. You are twenty-three, educated, a woman of independent means. Something else frightens you. Something else makes you run from me."

Her head spun, little spots danced before her eyes. She needed to exhale, inhale, but she couldn't, couldn't let go, couldn't admit what he said so freely, so carelessly.

She had been hurt by a man, violently hurt, and she was afraid of men. But that wasn't why she feared Kalen. She feared Kalen because what she wanted from him, needed from him, he would never give her.

She was looking for stability, security, permanence. He didn't commit.

She wanted love. He wanted sexual conquest.

She needed optimism and he was the most cynical man she'd ever met.

Now he was tipping her head back, revealing her throat. She shuddered again, feeling so damn exposed. Exposed physically, exposed emotionally.

Her gaze swept his high strong forehead, the hard slant of cheekbone, the firm jaw with firmer chin. Immovable. Resolute. How many times she'd dreamed about him, how many times she'd closed her eyes, pictured him, held his face and voice close? How many times she'd tried to recall every word she'd ever heard him say...

All those deferred hopes and dreams. Hopes, youthful hopes, girlish dreams.

The past broke her heart, just as it had once physically broken her. *"Kalen."*

Her voice cracked, anguished.

"There," he said, brow suddenly furrowing, his

gaze fixed, hawklike in its intensity. "There is the fear. It's real. It's puzzling."

Blood surged to her cheeks. Her mouth trembled. "It is real because I can't be your mistress. I can't be your plaything. It's not fair, Kalen. It's not fair to me." He was right, she was scared, scared of all the need inside her that she didn't know what to do with, didn't know how to reconcile herself to. Needs made one vulnerable, needs allowed one to be broken.

"Life isn't fair. But I can make it more equitable."

"Yet what you propose makes it less equitable."

His lashes lowered, his gaze drifted slowly across her upturned face. There was heat in his eyes, a heat that lit every inch of her skin. She could almost see herself the way he saw her and it wound her tighter on the inside. She needed more, wanted to be closer.

And then he was wrapping an arm around her and pulling her toward him, drawing her firmly against his body, making her impossibly aware of him—his size, his height, his superior strength.

She tried to ignore the crazy sensations flooding her, but he was warm, and hard, big, solid and everything inside her responded, heart racing, pulse pounding, body growing dangerously weak. Torture, this was torture.

"I want you," he said. "Very, very much."

Keira shook her head, surprised by the threat of tears. She didn't think she'd ever have the attention of a man like Kalen Nuri. After all, why would Kalen Nuri be interested in her? He was hugely successful, wealthy, powerful, literally a force to be reckoned with.

Even if he were poor, without the famous name and intimidating reputation, he could still have anyone with that face of his. He was more than handsome, he had something in his face, something in his eyes that rendered her helpless.

When he was in the room she was aware of him and only him.

When he looked at her every rational thought left her head.

Like now. She couldn't think, couldn't breathe.

Fire, she thought, fire, and there's not enough water to put it out.

She looked wonderingly into his face, wanting, and simultaneously fearful, knots forming in her tummy, the bite of adrenaline.

"We will take it slow," he said, holding her securely. "One step at a time."

One step at a time...just what did that mean?

A kiss...a touch...seduction...consummation... then what? One step at a time and where would this go? And what would happen when it was over?

She couldn't see the future, didn't know what

would happen even the day after tomorrow, but she knew she wanted Kalen, knew she felt desire unlike any desire she'd known before.

What to do with this desire? How to answer the fierce craving? Would it ever go away?

"One step," he repeated.

Her head swam. She wanted him. Wanted more of him, wanted to tip his head down to hers, wanted to feel the warmth of him, wanted to learn all that she could about him.

Would he still smell of spice?

Would he again taste like gold and sunshine? Would he be warm like the desert, or cool and crisp like the North African coast in winter?

"You've gone quiet on me," he said as he slid his thumb across her mouth, and her lips quivered to life, even as her tummy flipped inside out.

"I wasn't sure what I should say." Her voice came out breathy, faint.

"Yes, Kalen. That's all you have to say."

He would break her heart into a thousand pieces. She had to go. Today. Tonight. The first opportunity that presented itself.

Leaving him would hurt. But she smiled, despite the pain. "If I said yes to everything I'd be in trouble."

Heat blazed in his eyes. A muscle pulled in his jaw. "But life would be an adventure. And you, *laeela,* must like adventure because you've been searching for something a very long time."

Her eyes burned. Her mouth quivered, and the quiver drew his attention, and again he caressed her lower lip. Sensation rocketed through her, sharp, intense, and she must have made some inarticulate sound because his mouth quirked. "You will be fun to play with, *laeela.*"

Then his head lowered and his mouth briefly covered hers, a hard demanding kiss that parted her lips, demanded she give herself over to him. "You still resist," he murmured against her lips.

"I have to."

"No, you don't." He kissed her again, more gently, less pressure and the unexpected tenderness of the kiss took her breath away.

For a moment she felt so safe. For a moment she wanted to reach for him, wanting to hold fast to what seemed good and kind in him because she knew somewhere in him there had to be goodness and kindness.

Emotion rose, hot, stinging, hungry and her lips trembled beneath his. For a split second she let herself lean into him, let herself feel how hard he was, how strong, how confident. It was a hint of heaven, a taste of bliss. His mouth on hers, his arms around her, his strength supporting her.

Would she ever find what she was looking for?

Was there happiness on the other side of the rainbow?

The longing to love and be loved was so strong she felt almost suffocated by it. Was it wrong to feel so much? Did others ever feel this way?

Kalen lifted his head and his brow was furrowed, strong lines etched on either side of his mouth. "You are very hard to leave."

She felt a pang so bittersweet she bit down hard on the inside of her lip. If only that were true. If only he wanted her for her sake. But this was about power, this was about politics, this was a rich man's game. This is why she was leaving. "Is that one of your standard goodbye lines?"

He drew back, his expression suddenly fierce. "You insult me."

"I'm just trying to keep things honest."

Just trying to keep things honest.

Keira's words echoed inside Kalen's head, a sharp prick to his conscience.

Suddenly his two lives—the public and the private—felt dangerously close to colliding. She just wanted to keep things honest. The corner of his mouth lifted, tugged into a mocking smile by the impossibility of the situation.

She was so open, so candid, and he was all subterfuge. Cloak and dagger games.

Blood roared through his ears, the blood pumping hot and strong in his veins.

He wanted her, desired her, and knew if he made her his, he'd ruin her. Shame her. Shame her family.

And that had been the plan.

It still was.

He'd known from the beginning that he had to do this—had to make certain that Keira was undesirable, unmarriageable—and yet he knew she'd never been intimate with a man. He wasn't sure how he knew, but he recognized her momentary lapses, the glimpse of confusion in her eyes, the physical awkwardness. She'd been kissed before, touched, but never touched—or loved—the way he wanted to love her.

But he wasn't going to love her. He was going to hurt her. Shame her. He was the villain here, every bit as ruthless as Ahmed Abizhaid.

"We should at least be honest with each other," she added faintly, and yet her dark blue gaze met his, direct, steady, disarmingly steady. On one hand she spoke of fear, of her fear of him, and yet she spoke with the confidence of a woman that knew her mind. That spoke her thoughts freely.

Barakan, and Western.

A stolen curio from his world. And for a moment he considered her in that former life of his, the life of a man with unlimited time on his hands, the life of a man who was to rule the mountain tribes, a man with a huge territory, a territory still waiting on the North African continent for the ruler to return.

Then Kalen thought of Malik, pictured his young nephews and his resolve hardened.

He'd finish what he started. There was a reason he was who he was. There was a reason he did what he did.

"If you want honesty, *laeela,* I'll give you some. Learn to speak for yourself. Not for me." And he turned away before he could see the hurt register in her face, not wanting to see the pain in her eyes.

The harshness of Kalen's answer took her breath away and the tears she'd been fighting suddenly welled up.

And then Kalen's footsteps echoed. She looked up, caught sight of his back. He was walking away.

Kalen Nuri. Hope. Dream. Fantasy.

And she wanted the fantasy. Still. She wanted the fantasy more than she'd ever wanted anything, more than she should want anything.

But she didn't know what to say to him, couldn't call to him, couldn't say whatever it was that needed to be said. Instead she watched him walk through the hall and out the front door and then heard the door close.

It's better this way, she told herself, fighting off the threat of tears. Better for him to leave angry. Better for you to remain angry.

It'll be easier to leave.

You'll have more strength this way. Don't think about Kalen. Think about yourself. Think about your life. Think about survival.

And then the doorbell rang and Keira's heart lurched, a drunken lurch of hope and need.

Maybe he'd come back to apologize. Maybe he did care, care more than he could admit. Maybe this thing between them wasn't just about politics and power.

Impulsively Keira opened the front door before the butler could appear. And as the door opened her uncertain smile gave way to confusion, shock, and then understanding.

By the time she opened her mouth to cry for help, it was too late.

Across the city, Kalen had turned his phone off for his dinner meetings.

He knew what was happening back at the penthouse. He knew because he'd laid the trap.

He'd allowed them to be followed today, knew that he and Keira were being watched, saw the men trailing them, knew they'd been shadowed back to the penthouse.

And then he'd made a big show of leaving. Let the fight happen and deliberately walked out, leaving chaos in his wake.

He'd even pulled his security making the building vulnerable.

Leaving Keira exposed.

His meetings tonight went well—a smart cover—and yet they'd run long. A happy coincidence. Now at eleven with the last of the investors put in cabs for their respective hotels, Kalen headed for his own limousine.

"Where to, sir?" his driver asked him, holding the door open for him.

"The penthouse," Kalen answered, settling in the back.

Fifteen minutes later the limousine pulled up to the soaring apartment building. Police cars barricaded the entrance and the front door had been sealed off.

Something had happened.

Kalen climbed from the back of the limousine, and stood next to the car, assessing the situation.

Then he spotted his butler, Mr. Wellings, speaking with two men who were taking notes. Detectives, Kalen surmised.

More lights flashed and turning to look behind

him, Kalen spotted the growing throng of photographers and television cameras.

Headline news.

His gut twisted, his chest tight with inarticulate emotion. He hadn't expected the remorse. Or the emotion.

He set off, heading for Mr. Wellings and the detectives. "Your Excellency," the butler said. "I'm so sorry. I tried to phone. She's gone."

It had happened. Omar al-Issidri had reclaimed his daughter.

Just the way Kalen had planned.

CHAPTER SEVEN

IN THE back of the tinted Mercedes sedan, the men identified themselves as working for her father.

She wasn't surprised. They either had to work for her father or Ahmed Abizhaid, and if one had to pick between two evils—or as Kalen said, pick your poison—her father was preferable.

As the sedan headed for the airport, one of the men thrust a robe and headcloth at her. "Cover yourself," she was told disdainfully.

She didn't like his attitude or tone, but she did as he directed. It wasn't as if she had much choice. And other than that first, early directive, there was no other conversation as they drove to the private air terminal the international elite preferred.

Apparently the flight plan had been approved earlier and they departed immediately, flying straight from London to the most northern tip of the African continent.

Keira didn't sleep on the flight. Instead her thoughts circled round and round and the only thing she knew with any certainty was that her life was about to change. Yet again.

By the time dawn arrived she was exhausted but dry-eyed. As the sun rose, she stared out the window, watched the sun touch the vast sea of white-gold sand below the plane. It was so bright outside, the rising sun shining brilliantly, reflecting even more brilliantly off the jet's silver-white wings.

She was served a glass of juice and a pastry, then the jet banked to the right and made its final descent, landing at a private airstrip bordered by water and sand. She wondered where they were— Dubai, maybe?—before they transferred quickly from jet to helicopter.

The helicopter was large, seated six comfortably and after taking off, they again crossed miles and miles of sand, then over ridges of mountains, before the mountains gave way to a green valley, more mountains, the highest peaks still dusted with snow, before all finally became flat and beige again. More sand.

Now they were descending, straight down, landing in a remote corner of Baraka, a corner sandwiched between the Atlas Mountains and the border of Oahua, an independent Berber territory that no government had tamed, although many had tried.

On the ground, as the helicopter door opened, Keira was greeted by a blast of blistering heat. Her escorts urged her forward as hot stinging sand swirled across the small flat space that served as a landing pad.

She adjusted her head covering and as she stood there, sheets of sand danced before her eyes. A gathering of desert nomads, she thought, holding tight to the scarf covering her mouth, ghosts shaped from the palest grains of sand.

It was an unearthly sensation, being here, back in Baraka, standing in the middle of nowhere while silhouettes of sand rose and fell before her eyes.

But the trip wasn't over yet. Robed men waited with camels. She was to travel on.

Her chest squeezed, compressing with inarticulate emotion. Approaching the camels, she had to duck her head as the wind sharpened, howled, changed direction.

Climbing onto the kneeling camel's back, swirling sand rushed at her, the wind penetrating her scarf, filling her eyes, her nose, her mouth with grit. She spluttered, coughed, and coughed again. Her eyes streamed with painful tears.

She was back. Baraka. Land of a thousand dreams.

Land of a thousand nightmares.

The past slammed her, the confinement, the walls,

the lack of freedom. Her memories of Baraka were anything but happy.

She adjusted her weight on the camel's back, trying to ignore the prickly wool blanket as it itched her skin, trying to find a comfortable spot on the camel's hard, bony back.

The camel driver prodded the animal to its feet. Keira clutched the saddle horn, an attempt to steady herself as the camel lurched forward, a long drunken step. Her stomach lurched just as wildly.

Her father had flown her to the ends of the earth…miles from the civilized world of Atiq.

He'd isolated her intentionally, keeping her from family, friends, assistance. Whatever happened next was not going to be good.

"It's not good," the Sultan Malik Nuri said, speaking from his palace in Atiq to his brother Kalen on the phone. "You've created an international scandal…pushed Baraka into the news…in the most unflattering light possible, too."

Kalen, still in London, was quite familiar with the news. He should be. He'd created it. "It'll blow over."

"Not if you do what I know you intend to do."

"Abizhaid has been a threat for years."

"You can't just eliminate him." Malik sighed and Kalen could picture his older brother closing his eyes, pinching the bridge of his regal nose. "Not without just cause."

"There is cause—"

"I'm not talking about suspicions—"

"Neither am I. He was behind the attack on you five years ago. He masterminded the assassination attempt and he's gotten away with it."

"You've no proof."

"You trust too easily."

"And you not enough."

Kalen's upper lip curled. "That is why we have different jobs."

Malik was quiet, and when he spoke his tone was grave. "What about the girl?" He paused. "Her father wants reparation."

"Nothing happened."

"Don't be obtuse. You know you've ruined her. Dishonored a young woman from a good family. Dishonored daughter and father. Who will have her now?"

Kalen didn't answer. The silence stretched long. "I know she's in danger," he said finally. "I've made plans."

"Abizhaid wants her punished."

What Malik was saying without using the exact words was that in their culture, according to custom, Keira would be expected to restore family honor. If not through marriage, then through death.

"She should have never been used as bait," Malik added after a long silence. "If she is harmed—"

"She won't be."

"I'm prepared to intervene—"

"You won't have to. I know what I'm doing."

Keira sat up from the mattress bed on the floor of the tent, dragged her knees forward until they were pressed to her chest.

One day, she silently counted, twisting her robe over her knees, two days, three days. She'd been here three days now. Three days of isolation. Three days of endless silence.

She'd spent summers in Baraka, summers where she studied the language, attended private religion classes, summers of being cloaked, covered, despite the intense heat, summers where she visited old museums and learned of the historical significance of each of the ancient artifacts, but she'd never known this Baraka of tents and caravans, camels and nomads.

She'd never spent time beyond the Atlas Mountains, had never woken in a desert tent with the sky a curdling blood-red at dawn and the wind whipping at the canvas and sheepskin awnings.

Baraka had always seemed so foreign to her, so alien after England's pastoral cool, and yet this desert, so brown and barren which stretched endlessly in every direction was even more alien.

Here in the desert, she felt like one of the gnarled ironwood trees eking out survival in impossibly dry soil.

Her days in the tent had been odd, strange and disorienting. No one here told her anything. Of course she only saw the women, the men and women were segregated, and the few men in camp were distant, always on the periphery, standing watch although none was visibly armed. The women weren't rude. If anything, they seemed shyly curious, dark eyes friendly behind their veils, but they didn't talk.

She'd attempted conversation on several different occasions but each time had been discouraged by one or another of the women.

Their silence spoke volumes and it crossed her mind that she should be afraid. But she wasn't afraid. Just lonely.

And regretful.

The fantasy was just a fantasy. Not even Kalen Nuri, handsome sheikh, had been able to save her.

Everything she'd felt, everything she'd dreamed, was over.

No, don't think, she told herself, hugging her knees even closer. It's too late for that. Be smart. Don't want. Don't feel.

Abruptly the canvas tent flap was drawn back, bright sunlight streamed into the tent and Keira blinked, dazzled by the intense light outside. A tall thin bearded man entered the tent.

Keira scrambled to her feet. She'd recognize her father anywhere. She rushed toward him and then stopped. He'd aged twenty years in the past seven and Keira stared at him wonderingly. He'd grown frail, his arms thin beneath his simple *jellaba,* his beard more white than gray. "Father."

He said nothing, his thin features devoid of expression.

Her eyes burned. She stepped forward again and then didn't know what to do. They'd become strangers over the years. "You've been ill."

"What have you done to us?" he demanded, his voice low, harsh. It was as if she'd never spoken. "Have you no shame?"

His fury blistered, even as the heat and stinging desert wind. She should have expected this. "I'm sorry."

"Sorry does not redeem your honor. Sorry does not restore my name."

She bowed her head, bit her tongue. Maybe if she let her father speak, maybe if he vented his anger…

"There are consequences, daughter. There must be consequences."

"Am I to be punished?"

"Yes."

She needed to stay calm. "What do you intend to do?"

"It is for Sidi Abizhaid to decide. He was your betrothed."

She stared at her father, unable to speak.

"You shamed him, too, daughter. You have destroyed all our good names. All the good in our lives."

"Father, do not do this, do not let him choose—"

"I would be no more merciful."

"But you are my father. You have loved me from birth."

"I loved you before birth. I loved you when you were but a seed, an idea in your mother's mind and mine. But this is Baraka and your betrothed is powerful. Political. He was not one you could humiliate."

Her lips parted, but no sound came out.

"This is not easy for me," her father continued. "I have spent the past three nights praying. Fasting. I have spent the past three nights asking God for guidance—"

"Then help me, Father. Protect me."

"Abizhaid demands retribution. He will have his," her father paused, considered his words, "just as I will have mine."

"Revenge, Father? On whom?" But she knew, of course she knew. There was no love lost between her father and Kalen.

"Sheikh Nuri will suffer. Do not think you suffer alone."

After her father left, Keira stood in the middle of the tent, heart pounding wildly, stomach roiling with acid.

She knew what punished meant. She'd heard stories of girls punished for immorality.

And Kalen, what would her father do to him?

She shied away from the thought, unable to contemplate Kalen hurt, wounded, or suffering.

Keira left the tent, slipping beneath the flap. No one tried to stop her. A new tent had been erected, a large tent far more luxurious than her own.

That was where her father was.

Keira entered his tent, found her father just sitting down to a table where his books and papers waited.

"Father."

She'd startled him and he jumped. Anger showed in his face. "What are you doing here?" he demanded, motioning to the entrance. "I didn't give you permission to enter."

"You can't hurt Sheikh Nuri." Keira planted herself before her father's chair. "He's done nothing wrong."

"Nothing wrong? He dishonored you. Violated you—"

"He never touched me."

Her father fell silent, eyebrows beetling.

"We've never been intimate. The sheikh could have taken advantage of me, but he didn't." She felt herself flush. "He respected me."

Omar spat in disgust. "Kalen Nuri respects no one."

"But Sheikh Nuri respected me," she repeated stubbornly. "He respected my inexperience."

Her father's brow was as creased as a dry riverbed. He studied her for a long agonizing minute. "You're still a virgin then?"

A virgin. No, Dad, she wanted to say, I haven't been a virgin since I was raped. But she'd never told anyone about that night. Had suffered in silence instead.

In the beginning it had been her secret, and then later wore the stain like a badge of honor.

She was ruined.

No longer prized, or precious. A woman without value.

Omar shifted forward in his chair and reaching for her, he took her chin in his hand, held her face securely before his. "I asked you, are you still a virgin then?"

The two-hundred-thousand-dollar question.

How to answer? What to say? The truth, what was the truth anyway?

What was it she and Kalen had said days ago, that last conversation they'd had about honesty? She couldn't speak for anyone else. She could only speak for herself and she'd been attacked, not loved. There hadn't been sex but violence. Here she was, twenty-three, and she'd never made love, never known a lover's kindness, passion, or tenderness.

Her eyes burned. Her heart twisted, the ache of pain and hurt so strong she felt dangerously close to tears. "Yes," she answered, voice breaking, growing husky. "I am."

Her father's eyes gleamed. "You're certain?"

Certain? Certain that she'd been hurt? Certain that she'd been violated? Certain that she'd never been loved? "Yes."

His grip eased slightly. "You'd be willing to submit to a physical examination?"

She exhaled in a short, shocked puff. Keira tried to draw away but he wouldn't release her. *"What?"*

"If you're innocent…?"

She was shocked, but not. This was Baraka, after all. "My word's not good enough?"

"If you're still innocent you should have nothing to fear."

"I'm not afraid. Just disgusted."

"It's a matter of *hshuma*," he said, finally letting her go.

Shame, she repeated silently, backing away a step.

"It's reasonable for me to want to defend your name," her father continued, "reasonable to defend our family name. It's the only way to lift the *hshuma* that has darkened our reputation."

Icy with cold, Keira took another step backward. She crossed her arms over her chest, trying not to think about what her father was asking of her. "And if I do this…agree to be examined…this will clear Sheikh Kalen's name, too?"

"That's not for me to decide."

"Why not? You said you were the one that wanted to settle the score with Sheikh Kalen."

Her father snapped his fingers. "Enough. You care too much about a man that cares too little for you. Now go. I have arrangements to make." His thin lips pulled. "A doctor to send for."

With her father's words ringing in her head, Keira staggered back to her tent. What had she just done?

What had she just agreed to?

She couldn't prove she was still a virgin. There was no way in hell she'd ever be a virgin again.

Frantically she paced the red patterned carpet

in her tent, even as she put a hand to her stomach, feeling ill.

What was she thinking, telling her father she'd submit to the test? What was she thinking, delaying the inevitable?

Some wrongs, she thought, fighting to keep her stomach from heaving, couldn't be righted. No matter what one did. No matter how hard one tried.

Tears burned her eyes. Her throat felt raw as she forced herself to swallow. Slowly she sat down, falling to her knees in the middle of a mound of pillows on the red wool carpet.

She had to tell her father the truth.

She'd tell him what happened, how it happened, try to make him understand what took place all those years ago...

Perhaps her father would forgive her. Perhaps Ahmed would, too.

It wasn't as if she couldn't have children.

It wasn't as if she were truly used goods.

But it wasn't going to be easy, telling her father, not when he placed such a high value on purity. Innocence.

Not when her reputation was more precious to him than gold.

Hshuma, she silently said.

Hshuma, or shame, didn't exist in the West the

way it did in Baraka. In the West people might feel guilt over having done something wrong, but in Baraka guilt is non-existent, instead there is *hshuma*—shame—that others know that one has done something wrong. And in Baraka, honor and dignity were all important, the dignity surrounding one's name just as vital. For others to know about one's mistakes would be tantamount to disaster.

The difficult thing was that she understood this, had grown up with a foot in each culture and while her father couldn't understand her perspective, she did understand his.

Hshuma was the worst thing that could happen in their culture, it resulted in ostracism. And family members were held accountable for each other's actions.

Thus her father's desperation to clear their name.

But there was no miracle great enough to undo what had been done when she was sixteen.

By the time Kalen boarded his jet for Baraka, he knew everything he wanted to know. And more.

His contacts were reliable, his connections impeccable. After all, he was a sheikh, the second highest ranking noble in Baraka, descended from one of the oldest Berber tribes. It was his Berber blood that stood him in good stead now.

His Berber tribesmen reported back that Keira was being held at an encampment not far from the Ouaha border.

Ouaha, Arabic for oasis, meant something where there is nothing, and it was a fitting name for an independent territory bordered on one side by Baraka and the other by Algeria.

Throughout history many sultans and kings had attempted to annex Ouaha to their own country. And until twenty years ago Ouaha had been relentlessly attacked, assaulted, a place and people constantly under siege. But the Berbers were proud, fierce, and they fought for their survival, fought so valiantly that Kalen's late grandfather, Sherif Nuri, the reigning Sultan of Baraka, a Berber himself, had stepped in, promised Ouaha his support, guaranteeing the territory continued independence.

Sultan Sherif's support saved Ouaha, and resulted in his assassination.

The Berbers never forgot Sherif Nuri's sacrifice and years later when their stability again appeared threatened, the Berber leader claimed the Nuri heirs as their own. It was a strategic move. A wise move.

Malik, by then, was already the Sultan of Baraka.

Kalen, by virtue of being second son, inherited

the mantle of leadership. Kalen Nuri, sheikh of Baraka, became Sultan of Ouaha.

The Sultan title was honorary. There was no job description attached to the title, just the kasbah, a beautiful fortified castle on the slope of a mountain made from the same red rock and clay, a small income, and the loyalty of the people.

It was the loyalty Kalen valued most, particularly after the attempt on Malik's life five years ago. When Kalen asked the Berber tribesmen to keep their ears open, to report any whispers of responsibility, or rumblings of political discontent, they did.

Kalen knew more than anyone realized, had consolidated his power beyond what anyone imagined. Ouaha allowed him his secrets, his space. In Ouaha he was like a shadow. He could come and go and no one paid him any notice. And it was to Ouaha he went now.

The large caravan arrived on day six and the quiet camp was suddenly transformed into a bustle of activity. Keira parted the flaps of her tent to watch the caravan's arrival. There were many camels, many men.

Men from their camp called out to men arriving. Ritual greetings, Keira noted, catching bits of the conversation swirling around her, nearly all the talk about the camels' personalities, how the camels fared on the journey, which camels were worthless and how some were worth their weight in gold.

She'd learned years ago that in Arabic there were ten words to describe camels in their various ages and stages of growth, and she heard those words bantered about now. This camel was *hawer,* the infant, while this one over there was *jamal,* or fully grown.

Suddenly her father appeared and he was bowing to one of the men. The two talked briefly and then her father gestured to her tent.

Keira's heart stopped, squeezed.

It was either the doctor, or Ahmed Abizhaid. Perhaps the caravan brought both.

Fear and loathing washed over her and she dropped the flap, ducked back into her tent. Where could she go? What could she do? There had to be a way out somehow...

Hands on her hips, pulse pounding, she gazed around, saw what she had seen for the last six days. Fabric walls. A sheepskin bed. Scattered pillows on the floor. At night they lit candles.

What was she going to do? Burn the damn tent down? Grab a camel and jump on, making a mad dash for freedom into the desert night?

Great for a spy thriller but hardly practical.

The flap to her tent lifted. Her father stood there. He was smiling. Broadly. "He's arrived," her father announced, giving his beard a tug of satisfaction.

She felt only horror. "He?" she whispered, her blood turning to ice, her limbs freezing cold.

"The doctor." He paused for effect. "And I've more good news."

"More?"

Her father's smile grew. "Sidi Abizhaid is on his way."

Keira sat in her tent, on one of the low leather and wood stools waiting for the doctor to arrive.

Don't think, she told herself. Don't think, don't want, don't feel.

But how not to feel when her emotions were so chaotic, fear and anger so jumbled inside of her? Her father had no right. She was not a possession. She was a woman. Her body belonged to no one but herself...

The examination was a violation. A betrayal of trust. A shattering of innocence.

She tried to tell herself she'd survived worse, tried to remind herself that this exam was medical, not personal, that it'd be brief. Matter of fact.

Uncomfortable.

Her eyes burned, the back of her throat raw with all the suppressed emotion.

She couldn't do this. She couldn't bear to be touched by strangers…but did she have a choice? Could she prevent this?

No.

And maybe this was for the best. Maybe it was time her father knew the truth about what happened that night when she was sixteen. Maybe it was time she stopped running from her past.

Keira pressed her forehead to her knees, suddenly very tired. She felt as if she'd been running for a long time, running to escape the loneliness and shadows of her childhood.

The loneliness had haunted her.

She'd felt absolutely torn between her parents, their conflicting cultures, her own mixed ethnic makeup. On the outside she didn't look so different—she'd inherited her mother's coloring, pale ivory skin, deep blue eyes—but on the inside, she wasn't really, truly English, not in the way the girls she knew were.

Growing up, her mother would periodically invite other couples over, families with mixed races, and her mother would smile and gesture grandly as if to say, "there you go, mixed children, are you happy now?"

Her mother, her brilliant, free-thinking Anglo-Irish mother had never understood. It was one thing to invite someone of mixed ethnicity over for dinner. It was another to be different yourself.

Lonely. Yes. She'd been lonely, and the loneliness was the sort that did not devour you whole, but rather in hard insistent bites, one after the other. The bite of being an only child. The bite of having two homes. The bite of her mother remarrying. The bite of her father's disapproval as she became the Western daughter he'd never wanted.

You'll get through this, she told herself now, just as you've gotten through everything else. It's going to be fine.

But in her heart of hearts she knew it wasn't fine. Once the news was out, nothing would ever be fine again.

Voices pierced her cloud of misery. People had entered her tent.

"Keira." Her father said her name. "The doctor is here."

She felt a hot lance of pain, high in her chest, a cut through her heart, all the way down to her middle. Slowly she lifted her head, looked past her father to the small group behind him. Tears filled her eyes. "Do not make me do this, Father."

"The women will shield you," he said, indicating the two veiled women accompanying the doctor.

"The exam will be brief. Discrete. You will not be alone. Sidi Abizhaid and I will wait outside."

"Sidi Abizhaid has arrived then?"

"Yes. He's taking tea in his tent, but he is most anxious for the results of the examination."

"Father."

He ignored her agonized protest. "It's best to just proceed quickly. Get this unpleasant task behind us." Omar gestured for the physician. "Doctor?"

The doctor and the veiled women moved forward. Keira trembled. Black spots danced before her eyes. She couldn't do this, couldn't let them touch her.

One of the women began to unfold a blanket. "You will be covered, *Lalla* al-Issidri," the doctor said respectfully.

"No." Keira couldn't move from her stool. "I cannot do this."

"It will take just a few minutes—"

"No," she choked.

"No," a male voice echoed her protest, the tent flap opening, falling.

She knew the voice. Knew it as surely as she knew her own and yet it couldn't be, the timing was too improbable, miracles didn't happen like this...

"Do not lay a hand on her," he was still speaking

and Keira stared in fascination as Kalen strode forward, garbed in a white robe, his black hair covered by a white headcloth, his features a mask of cold fury. "I will kill the man that touches what is mine."

CHAPTER EIGHT

"BUT she isn't yours," her father roared, caught off guard, but not about to yield. "She is promised to Sidi Abizhaid. Sidi Abizhaid paid the bride price—"

"Return it then."

"I cannot."

Kalen shrugged, as calm as Omar was furious. "You've no choice. I've already laid claim to your daughter."

"She said nothing happened." Omar smashed one hand into the other. "She said you hadn't touched her."

Kalen didn't bother to answer. He'd already turned to Keira, and in his white robe, with his hands on his hips, he looked fierce. Hard. Savage. "Have you been hurt?"

Her heart still thudded too hard. She didn't understand what was happening or where this was leading. "No."

He wasn't satisfied. "Have you been mistreated in any way?"

Her sheikh was looking for a fight, she thought, muscles weak from too much adrenaline. "No."

Her father jabbed his finger at Kalen. "Enough of this. You've no business here. Nor any claim on my daughter. Sidi Abizhaid is to marry Keira tomorrow."

"Unlikely, Sidi al-Issidri," Kalen was practically smirking, "as your daughter is already married to me."

What?

Keira's heart jumped, squeezed, feeling like a little rubber ball lodged in her throat.

Married to Kalen Nuri? The second most powerful man in Baraka? One of the world's richest, most eligible men?

No one in his position would ever marry someone like her, and yet the words dazzled and she choked, thinking of the night in Dallas when he'd appeared on the balcony at the party. She'd been stunned to see him. Stunned and yet thrilled.

And now he was here and the thrill was even worse. Sharper. Stronger. Far too alive.

Her father found the idea as ridiculous. "There's no way you've married. Keira would have told me. She would have said something."

"Not if I told her to keep it secret." Kalen lifted a hand, gestured toward her with one commanding finger. "Come," he said softly, "greet me, wife."

She'd never seen Kalen dressed in the traditional Barakan robes. She'd only ever seen him in slacks, dress shirts, the expensive Western wardrobe he wore. And yet now with his white robe belted, his headcloth covering nearly all of his dark hair, his hands on his hips, he looked every inch the powerful sheikh.

"She is not your wife!" Her father moved to grab her and Kalen stepped between.

"Step back." Kalen's husky voice rumbled a clear warning. He would not have Keira threatened in any way.

"You cannot have her. It won't happen."

"Too late."

"No. I would rather see her dea—"

"Careful," Kalen interrupted, voice dropping to a silky smoothness, even as murder gleamed in his eyes. "Harm so much as one hair on her head, and you will suffer. Endlessly. Tremendously. You will wish you'd never been born."

Silence filled the tent, silence and tension so thick that Keira shuddered inwardly with the weight of it.

Omar flushed, his voice came out strangled. "I am the Sultan's advisor and confidant—"

"The Sultan has blessed our marriage. He approves of the union."

Omar paled, ruddy red fading to ash. "Sidi Abizhaid will cut your throat."

Dark amusement glittered in Kalen's eyes. "I'd like to see him try."

Her father was running out of arguments. "And the bride price? What of that?"

"It'll be paid."

"For you it's double."

"Why not triple it, al-Issidri?" Kalen's voice was so low it sounded like a snarl. "Why not get as much as you can for your only child?"

Keira held her breath, awash in pain. In shame.

She felt like nothing, like a nonentity. Something you might see at the market. Something one would haggle over…

And then she exhaled, reminded herself that at this moment her feelings were secondary. What she had to do was stop this horrible battle between Kalen and her father. They couldn't continue like this. Her father had a temper, but Kalen was stronger, more powerful. Her father might lash out blindly, but Kalen would strike the jugular.

Her father might have power, but against Kalen, he didn't have a prayer.

"Stop," she said fiercely. "Stop this now. Please."

Her father looked at her, shock and anger in

his eyes. "Daughter, tell me you haven't married him."

"Wife, come to me," Kalen commanded.

"Keira. Daughter."

"Laeela."

Heart pounding, she glanced from one to the other. She was to choose, she realized. Choose her future. Choose her path. Right now, in this tent, in front of her father and the one man she'd hoped might be her lover.

This was crazy. Madness.

She felt the pressure building, the battle of wills, the assertion of ego, the fierce need for control.

She knew the past, she thought, but she didn't know the future. And it was the future she wanted.

"Keira," her father repeated and she looked at him for a long, level moment, sorrow for all that had never been, filling her. She shook her head faintly, apologetically.

And then with a nervous jingle, she settled the wide gold bracelets lower on her wrist and crossed to Kalen.

She'd chosen.

Kalen's predatory gaze missed nothing as Keira approached him. Not her uncertain step, nor the uneasy jiggle of her wrist, nor the tension at her mouth.

She was scared half to death and stood before Kalen, head bowed.

"Look at me," Kalen ordered.

She didn't want to look but she couldn't ignore the authority in his voice. He was too strong, too forceful. Little by little she lifted her head until the intensity in his eyes seared her, possessed her.

Heat filled her. Heat that only seemed to flare and grow.

"I would have hoped for a warmer greeting from my wife after seven days apart," he said.

She didn't miss his dark sardonic humor. Or the light of battle glinting in his eyes. He'd enjoyed the conflict. He'd be dangerous to cross. "Forgive me. *Husband.*"

She tacked on the last word, her tone not entirely respectful.

"No kiss for your husband?" Kalen taunted.

She blushed, her face hot, the top of her cheekbones tingling. "No." Her jaw jutted challengingly. "Husband."

Kalen smiled, his features as set. "I had forgotten how shy you are. Wife."

"If she is your wife," Omar said slyly.

Kalen's gaze never wavered from Keira's face. "She is. My wife. And my treasure."

Omar's laugh was bitter. "Then you have a most unwilling treasure. Just look at her," he continued, his tone sharp and needling. "She defies you. Not just in word, but in deed. She does not kiss you, acknowledge you, pay you proper respect."

Kalen shrugged. "She is still a new bride."

Her father cleared his throat. "I hate to call you a liar—"

"Then don't." Kalen spoke softly, and he smiled at Omar but there was nothing remotely kind, or forgiving, in his expression. "I would hate to make you eat your words. It would be quite...painful."

Rage lit Omar's eyes. "Perhaps I would not doubt the marriage if I had proof." He paused, allowed the silence to lengthen. "Perhaps my daughter would be more obedient, if the ties to you were more binding."

"They are binding enough."

"Clearly, my daughter does not think so."

Kalen studied Keira's face for a long, thoughtful moment before looking at Omar. "You wish for a renewal of the vows?"

Omar's expression was equally flinty. "I want a wedding, yes."

"Then so it shall be," Kalen said. "Tonight we shall recite our vows—"

"No!" Keira couldn't keep her silence, couldn't allow this to continue on. The games, the pretense, the power, the positioning...they were using her, over and over, fighting each other with her as a weapon. "I will not be part of this. I will not be misused by either of you. You are not fair," she stormed. "Neither of you are fair. You haven't asked me. You haven't talked to me—"

"I told you she is unwilling. Far too rebellious." Omar sneered down his nose. "You must break her of that."

"Thank you for the advice." Kalen reached for her, a cynical smile playing at his lips, as his hand wrapped around her upper arm and brought her closer to his side. "But I enjoy my wife's fire. I would hate to break her...spirit."

His thumb caressed in slow circles on her arm, his touch warm, so warm, it made her pulse quicken, her nerves scream to life.

He was dangerous, she thought wildly, a man as hard on the outside as he was on the inside. A man that didn't care what anyone thought of him and cared even less about pleasing others.

Brave man. Proud man.

In her next life she'd like to come back like Kalen, would like to be strong. Hard. Indifferent to the opinions of others.

Impervious to the slings and arrows...

"Spirit is one thing. Disobedience is another. You will need patience to teach her to obey," her father added. "Patience and time."

A wicked gleam warmed Kalen's golden eyes.

"Yes," he agreed, siding with her father for the first time. "Your daughter is like a *ba'eer,* an adolescent camel, one not yet fully grown."

A camel? Had Kalen really just compared her to a camel?

But her father was nodding, as if Kalen had just uttered some pearl of wisdom. "And like a camel, she has an incredible memory. She will remember the lessons you teach her if you beat her now and then."

"Beat her?" Kalen repeated, still studying her intently. And then he shook his head. "No, I could never beat her. But then, I don't beat my camels, either. I don't believe one should use force against camels—or women. Instead, they must be persuaded to obey."

She flashed Kalen a look of loathing. He was as bad as her father! "How wonderful it is that the two of you can simplify life's problems by grouping women and camels in the same category."

Omar's brow creased. "I would begin the lessons promptly."

"I agree," Kalen replied. "But first I should speak to Abizhaid. Let him know how things are—"

"Do not," her father interrupted. "Let me handle this. I do not wish tonight's festivities to be marred by bloodshed."

Kalen half bowed. "Let Abizhaid know that I

have brought many men with me, many of the Sultan's guards. It would not be wise for him to do anything here. But Abizhaid is more than welcome to join us tonight. I'd like for him to witness our vows."

Omar returned Kalen's half bow and then turned and left.

Keira watched her father walk out, and it wasn't until the flap fell behind him that she realized the funny taste in her mouth was blood from biting her tongue so hard.

Fury filled her. She saw red. "Did you have to do that?" she demanded, facing Kalen, hands on her hips. "Was it necessary to humiliate me?"

"I didn't."

"You did. You made a fool out of me. Comparing me to a camel!"

The corner of his mouth quivered. He was trying not to laugh. "I thought your father would relate. And he did, didn't he? He warmed—"

"You don't even like my father."

He shrugged. "But soon he will be family."

She couldn't believe it. Couldn't believe he'd continue to scheme and manipulate her like this. "We're not getting married."

"But we are. Tonight. Didn't you hear us discuss the plans?"

"Kalen. You can't do this."

"I don't have a choice. It was the best way to protect you."

Her heart squeezed tight. She lifted her chin, defiantly. "You've lied to my father. Please don't lie to me, too."

He wasn't smiling anymore, all laughter gone. The tension inside her just grew. She wasn't sure what she wanted from him—a confession? Or a denial?

"You aren't here for me," she persisted. "This is just another strategic move on your part, isn't it?"

His broad shoulders shifted impatiently. "Your father drives a hard bargain. I did what I had to do."

"So you lied. You said we were married."

"Yes." He was utterly unapologetic.

"You don't mind lying?"

"I mind violence. I mind civil unrest. I mind a plot to assassinate a king and his children."

"But you don't mind hurting me."

"This isn't about you."

"No. Of course not. Silly me." She'd wanted the admission but now that he said it, she felt sick. Her stomach knotted. Her heart raced. Even her hands felt cold and damp. Completely heartsick.

"So tell me about our wedding. The one I seem

to have missed. What was it like? How did you propose?"

"It was a whirlwind engagement."

He was a bastard. "Love at first sight?"

His gaze moved leisurely across her face, touching briefly on her eyes, her cheeks, her mouth before dropping lower, drifting down, breasts, belly, hips, thighs. "Or lust. Your choice."

Lust. Interesting word.

She had lusted after him once. She still felt tremendous desire. "And where were we when we said these vows? In a church, or was it a civil ceremony?"

"A civil ceremony. It was very rushed."

"And was I happy?"

His gaze held hers, amusement lurking in the golden depths. "Ecstatic. But then you did not have much choice in the matter. I wanted you. I was determined to have you. Saying vows was just a formality."

His tone made a lump rise to her throat. Hot tears burned the back of her eyes. "You've created quite a story. Passionate. Romantic. Guaranteed to sweep any woman off her feet."

"Including you?"

How to answer that? He'd swept her off her feet years ago.

Kalen Nuri had been with her, buried so long in

her mind, carried so long in her heart, he was like part of her inner life, a private world no one saw, no one knew.

She'd clung to his memory and somehow his memory alone had kept her strong when nothing else seemed to matter, when the pain of the past and the uncertainty of the future overwhelmed her courage.

Kalen Nuri had been a touchstone. A landmark. A sweet memory to help her find her way home.

"And how do we get out of this web of deceit now?" she asked, feeling the air catch in her chest, a pocket of pain. "Because the lies are pretty thick. The trap is laid."

"We marry. We make good on our story."

Our story? His story. "I didn't want to be your mistress, Kalen. I certainly don't want to be your wife."

"Yet you'd be an ideal first wife."

Her fingers itched to slap him. His arrogance was insulting. "'First wife'?"

"Of course the number of wives is negotiable."

Camels. Wives. Kalen was certainly enjoying his trip home to the desert, wasn't he? "You and my father are eerily similar. Driven by different ideologies, but cut from the same cloth."

Kalen's eyes narrowed. "I'm nothing like your father."

"You are exactly like my father and you seem to be under the same mistaken impression that I'm a commodity on the market to be bartered and traded—"

"Never bartered, or traded. You are far too valuable for that."

Valuable, was she? Then why had she been treated like a stuffed doll, grabbed and dragged from one country to the other? Why was she back in Baraka when she'd sworn this was the last place she'd ever go? "If I was so valuable, *Your Excellency,* why didn't you protect me better? If I was so valuable, why didn't you secure your building…provide bodyguards…do whatever you could to make sure my father wouldn't take me?"

"You missed the strategy, *laeela.*" He leaned toward her, touched the tip of her nose with his finger. "Your father was supposed to take you."

She would have loved to bite his finger. "Say that again."

"I deliberately allowed your father access to my building in London. I fully expected him to take you." His hesitation was deliberate. "It was my… strategy."

His strategy. Again.

So that explained it. He hadn't been careless. He hadn't been oblivious. He'd been cruel.

He'd allowed her to be taken from his penthouse.

He'd wanted her to be forced into a strange car, and then a strange plane. It was his idea that she be hunted like a field mouse while the hawk pursued from the air.

The realization was like a blow to the head. Her lips parted. Her jaw moved. But she couldn't make a sound. Instead her mind sifted woozily through the various pieces of the puzzle, trying to see how any of it fit together and yet too stunned to come to the necessary conclusion.

Keira averted her head, exhaled in a short hard puff. She didn't think she could bear the hurt. He'd hurt her, disappointed her more than she'd ever thought possible. All these years she'd told herself not to ever want anything from a man, not to expect, not to need, but somehow, after spending a few days with Kalen, she'd hoped…

She'd wanted…

She'd dreamed…

She'd become exactly what her mother disparaged—a woman that needed a man.

Hadn't her mother always said, never need a man? And never, ever trust one? At least, never trust a man to want more of you than your butt and breasts, your hips, your thighs, your lips, your tongue?

Never trust him to want you for you, or your mind for your mind. They'll say they want you, say they love you, they'll say whatever they have to say to get you in bed, to get you to give them what they want. Sex. It's all about sex, dear, never forget.

And somehow Kalen had made her forget. Somehow she'd wanted to believe in fairy tales again, wanted to believe that knights in shining armor existed even though he said he left chivalry for the French and English.

She shouldn't have forgotten.

"Your idea of strategy, Kalen, was to allow me to be kidnapped...forced into marriage?"

"It was a matter of national security."

National security. Her lips lifted, a brittle smile of disbelief. "You, who cares so little for your nation that you moved to another country, changed your citizenship, severed all personal, economic and emotional ties, did this for national security?"

"As I said, the Sultan and his children had been threatened."

He was like a mountain. Tough. Rigid. Unyielding. He'd give her nothing. No sympathy, no warmth, no compassion.

This was about his brother, his family.

And she understood at one level. But at another, she didn't. Kalen had once been so huge in her world, so significant, that his *strategy* was the ultimate of betrayals. "Are they safe now?" she asked, voice husky, heart breaking.

"I hope so."

"Me, too." She looked away, blinked, reached up to wipe a slipping tear.

"So you understand."

Her lips stretched but the smile wouldn't come. "I understand you tricked me."

"No tricks involved."

Just deceit. Emotion burned inside her, emotion that made her eyes itch, her throat threaten to seal closed. "You could have told me."

"There are some things I tell no one."

Silence stretched, the silence feeling as heavy as death. She'd hoped, oh how she'd hoped, even when she'd told herself she wasn't hoping, even when she'd convinced herself she'd stopped hoping, that he might, just might, fall for her.

Fall in love with her.

Oh, the impossibility of hope, but hadn't hope driven civilization through thousands of years?

Didn't everyone secretly dream of—crave—one true love? The kind of love that answered yourself, the kind of love that said you, you're the one. The only one.

The other half.

The better half.

Two halves make a whole. Unity. Sanctuary.

"Keira, you are making too much of this."

She couldn't look at him. "Go."

"I wasn't going to let you marry him."

Her heart was too heavy. Her stomach churned, acid surging through her in unrelenting waves. "No? Are you sure?"

"I would have never let it happen."

Tears of shame and outrage burned so hotly she had to dig her nails into her palms to keep them from falling. "Well, when were you going to come? At what point were you going to call things off?" But the tears fell anyway. "When were you going to take control? On the first night of Ahmed's and my wedding celebrations? On the last night? Moments before he took me to bed? After he took me to bed? What were you going to do?"

"But I am here. I arrived when I was meant to arrive."

Confidence was one thing. Callousness was another. "How could you do that to me, Kalen?"

"You were safe."

"Safe?" She stepped back, swiped at the tears falling. "I wasn't safe. I was scared. I didn't know what was going to happen."

"But nothing bad happened."

Nothing? Maybe not in his world. But she'd suffered this past week, suffered in ways he'd never know, or understand. The absence of hope was the worst absence of all. One could take hunger, physical pain, thirst, one could suffer many agonies but to lose all hope…

It wasn't as if Kalen Nuri loved her, needed her or even wanted her. This was about politics. *Politics.*

"I will never marry you," she said roughly. "You can beat me like a camel, but I will never marry you. Never. Ever."

Kalen almost felt sorry for her. "I've no intention of beating you. There are other methods of persuasion, *laeela,* methods much more effective with one as passionate and sensitive as you."

She looked away, stared pointedly across the tent. Kalen felt a welling of sympathy. She belonged to him and she still didn't seem to know it.

His sense of possession was strong, almost primal. It had been a long time since he'd felt a tie to anyone other than his brother, and his brother's children.

But Keira. She was his. They might not have been physically intimate yet, but it didn't change the fact that she belonged to him. He flashed to the harems of his ancestors, the princes and sultans and sheikhs with their desert palaces and elegant harem quarters, rooms decorated in the finest copper, silver and gold with exquisite bathing pools tiled in fanciful mosaics. He would have her, know her, pleasure her, but first he needed to extricate them from this political minefield.

"We are marrying tonight. A real wedding," he said. "I've given your father my word."

Keira laughed; she could do nothing else. This was funny in a tortuous sort of way. Kalen had put her through hell and back and now he was dangling marriage in front of her like a damn carrot hanging from a stick. "No," she said softly. "No."

"Your father expects it."

"Too bad."

"He insists."

"Let him insist. Let him do what he wants, but I'd rather face punishment at his hands than continue this with you."

Kalen watched her with an almost clinical detachment. "You mean it."

"I do." Memory made her heart burn. Stung her eyes. Her throat felt swollen with weeks of tears. "I hate you."

"Hate?"

"With all my heart."

"And you've a big heart."

"Once." She drew a shallow breath. "Once I did."

CHAPTER NINE

HE LIFTED his hand, stroked the curve of her cheekbone.

Her lips parted, a silent gasp escaping. The touch was light but the sensation intense.

"I think you have missed me," he said, "more than you will admit."

"No."

She wasn't strong enough to let this conversation continue, hadn't the endurance to be so close and not be his. "I'll tell my father the truth," she said, gathering herself, realizing the break had to be made, and now. "He'll be angry, but it's better to let him know immediately, deal with the consequences up front."

"Keira."

"I'll tell him it's my fault. You go—"

"Keira."

She just talked faster, hoping to get the words out before she fell apart. "I never wanted this, never asked for this. It's time it ended now."

"I'm not going anywhere."

His head tipped, dark hair brushing the collar of his robe. His black hair had grown since she first met him that night in Dallas. It gleamed now in glossy waves, dense, thick, the polished sheen of onyx and her fingers itched to reach out, touch the length at his nape, the longer strands curling up against his collar.

But of course she wouldn't. He was gone. Dead to her. She'd have no part of him because if she let herself feel even a little, if she let herself feel one ounce of the want and need she'd once felt she'd fall apart. Self-destruct.

The virgin annihilation. Except she wasn't a virgin. Technically not a virgin.

"But I don't want you, Kalen, and I don't want to be married to you." She was trembling on the inside, the emotions so intense. He had to go. He had to leave now before she broke down. She wrapped her arms snugly across her chest, chilled despite the warm afternoon. "I don't ever want to see you again. I just want you to go and give me some peace."

"How could I leave you?" He sounded so reasonable, as if he were dealing with an exhausted child. "I've claimed you." He reached for her, hands on her shoulders, his hands sliding down over her arms. "You are mine. Forever."

Panic stirred within her, panic laced with desperation. He couldn't come any closer.

"No!" She tried to pull away, needing distance, needing peace, needing everything but what Kalen gave her.

Kalen checked a smile. He'd never been kept at such arm's length before. Yet he knew she wasn't unaffected by him, knew she felt the crackle of tension between them, the sharp hot flare of sexual heat.

He wanted her.

He would have her. Soon. Very soon.

Keira couldn't breathe. The air caught in her throat and her throat sealed closed.

It was hot, she thought, the tent was hot, the afternoon hot, the atmosphere too close, too intimate. "Should I send for tea?" she whispered, her mouth painfully dry, her heart beating frantically.

"No."

"You must be thirsty—"

"For this," he said, lifting her face to his, and his gaze searched her eyes before his mouth slowly covered hers.

The warm pressure of his mouth on hers was her undoing.

The warm steady pressure unleashed a firestorm of feeling within her, taking her pain, her anger and whipping it to something fiercely alive. He'd made her feel so much these past weeks, taken her from her home in Dallas, isolated her in this luxurious flat of his, dressed her up, paraded her around town, for what? To torture her father? To provoke a confrontation?

Emotion balled in her stomach, weighted her limbs and she couldn't stop Kalen, couldn't find the strength to tell him no when she welcomed the pressure of his mouth, the fury of the kiss. At least now she felt something concrete, felt something strong, physical, real. The words between them had only made things worse.

She needed this. She'd have this, take as much as she could from him, take until some of her pain went away.

He'd used her to get at her father. He was still using her. Maybe it was her turn to use him.

Her arm reached up, her wrist snaking around his neck. Her lips opened beneath his, her body trembling as she felt the first flick of his tongue across her lower lip.

His hands settled in the small of her back, his hands urging her closer, arching her backward so her hips pressed against his, her pelvis coming into intimate contact with his groin.

He felt hard, hot, taut, very aroused. She shuddered as her sensitive belly scraped his erection, shuddered again as everything inside her coiled, contracted.

She'd felt attracted to men before, felt curious about desire, but desire had never made her want to be in a man's arms, in a man's bed, her fear of pain greater than even the strongest curiosity. But with Kalen against her, Kalen kissing her, she couldn't think, couldn't remember her fears, couldn't remember anything but getting more... feeling more...drowning the senses in this heady, crazy sensation.

His hands traced the length of her spine, slowly covering every vertebra. She felt weak, liquid, her body melding into his, and each press of his hip, the brush of chest against her breast was like setting a match to dry kindling.

The heat between them flared hotter, the flames licking brighter, the desire as real and alive as the two of them. The desire as real and fierce as her pain had been.

He lifted his head, his lips inches from her, his breath warm on her face, his taste still in her mouth, the feel of his lips and tongue still imprinted on her mind.

He'd kissed her senseless, she thought dizzily. She had no thought left, no mind of her own.

"Yes, beloved?" he mocked, knowing she'd

given herself over to him, knowing she could hold nothing back from him.

Keira fought to gather her wits, quiet her senses. She wrapped her hands around his wrists. "Don't do this." The words were torn from her, her emotions still wildly stirred.

"You want me. You desire me. Stop fighting me."

"I might want you, but I don't want to be used. Not by you."

"I offer you protection. Sidi Abizhaid is dangerous."

"And you're not?"

He had the gall to smile. "It would be easier to submit to me, than him."

Submit.

How she hated the word and yet wasn't this what she'd done her entire life? Submit to her father? Submit to her mother?

Keira held her breath, the air bottling hot and sharp in her lungs.

"You've seen my life in London," he added. "You know I am progressive. Western. Married to me you'd have every opportunity. Advantages most people could only dream about."

"But I don't want advantages."

"What do you want then?"

The corner of her mouth tilted, the same crazy tilting she felt inside her, emotion sliding around like a roller-coaster ride. "Love." She looked up at him and the crooked smile faded. "It's obvious you need me. You might even want me. But you don't love me."

"Keira—"

"No. Stop telling me what I need. Let me tell you what I need. I need love, Kalen. I want love—"

His head dipped. He cut her words off with another kiss, this one surprisingly gentle. By the time he lifted his head, she was trembling, her legs jelly-like, her pulse frantic.

He cupped her cheek, stroked the flushed satin skin. "And haven't you yet learned, *laeela,* that we can't have everything we want?"

She stared up at him, tears filling her eyes. She hated him.

Hated him.

He was breaking her heart, destroying what was left of her dreams. "I will never forgive you." Her voice was but a whisper.

"It is a chance I take." His hand fell from her face. "The women will come to help you bathe and dress. Try to relax, Keira. It's a wedding, not an execution." And then he left.

* * *

Mummy. The word whispered through her head, her hands shaking as she fastened the ornate dangling gold earring to one lobe and then the other.

Mummy. She was wrapping herself up again. Mummy. She was putting herself back into the ground but this time she wasn't asleep. This time her eyes weren't closed. This time she was still breathing, still dreaming.

She was dressing for the wedding but it felt like her funeral. She'd wanted more, not less.

Don't think, she told herself, don't feel. Be the mummy you once were, the mummy you do so beautifully.

And gazing into the mirror she struggled to smile at the jeweled woman in a narrow cream pleated dress staring back at her. Long dark hair artfully tumbled. Elegant eyebrows that winged above dark eyes. Pale pink mouth. Pale ivory skin. Her fashionable pallor set off by the stunning shimmer of gold—gold at the ears, gold at the neck, gold at the wrists.

With her palms hennaed, her gown covered by a matching robe, there was nothing left to do but join Kalen.

Pausing in the opening of her tent, Keira used the moment to collect herself, but forgot everything as the landscape took her breath away.

The sun was beginning to set and tonight the

desert was beautiful, more than beautiful, with the big purple-blue sky extending in every direction over a sea of sand painted every shade of rose and gold. The scattered tents were almost too white beneath the sinking sun and the outdoor fires scented the air with rosemary and cumin, garlic and onion.

Lovely.

Her heart squeezed and she suddenly understood why there were those who couldn't live in the city, not after growing up in the desert. Here things were simple. Elemental. The heat and the sun, the wind storms that whipped the sand to a frenzy and the sudden stunning silence after the fierce winds had moved on.

She loved the white-hot glare of sky.

The burning winds, the roiling sands, the intense unyielding heat.

If things had been different she would have loved to call Baraka home…

And then her trance was broken as robed women moved toward Keira, talking animatedly, encircling her, providing her the appearance of community, stability.

During the brief, simple ceremony, Keira stood next to Kalen, her gaze fixed with seeming modesty on a spot in the middle of his white robe, her own ivory gown hidden by a long robe of similar color, her dark hair, loosely covered by an ivory silk scarf embroidered in silver and gold.

As the final binding words were said, the sun disappeared, sinking swiftly into the horizon's edge, turning the sky and sand a haunting bloodred.

A blessing was uttered and then Kalen leaned forward, kissed her on each cheek.

And that was it. "We're married?" she said, as the crowd surrounding them began wildly cheering and clapping.

"Husband and wife," he answered mockingly.

Husband and wife.

The feast after the ceremony went on late into the night, the dinner, and there were hours of entertainment, singing, dancing. The large tent was packed, filled with a standing room only crowd in the entry, and through it all, Keira sat at Kalen's side, trying to be nonchalant, trying to act as though he wasn't having such a disturbing effect on her senses, even though every nerve in her body clenched tight, every nerve aware of how he sat, how he moved, how close his shoulders, his hips, his thighs were to her.

Once she would have found Kalen's energy intense, exciting.

Once she would have given anything for him to look at her with a half smile playing at his mouth, fine lines creasing at the corners of his eyes. His expression tonight was sexy, sensual, indulgent, and once she would have wanted more, would have wanted him to keep looking at her, would have wanted him to want her...

But that was before she'd been made his wife. Now she knew she'd be forced to reveal her truth.

Her secret shame.

And then what would happen? How would Kalen react? Would he be angry? Disgusted?

Would he reject her?

Punish her?

Tell her father he'd unknowingly married used goods...

She drew a breath, eyes smarting, chest tight with pain. She must have made a sound because Kalen suddenly looked at her, eyebrows lowered, expression searching. "Are you well?" he asked.

He was concerned. His concern touched her.

She drew another quick breath, the pain growing brighter, hotter. She knew he wanted her. Knew that he intended to have her. Soon, very soon, probably tonight. "Yes, thank you. Just a little tired."

"It's been a long day."

She blinked hard, and nodded. It had been a very long day. Her emotions had been all over the place.

"Are you worried about tonight?"

Terrified, she silently answered, and yet she'd known they'd eventually come to this. She'd known from the start they were on this collision course.

"You're still so innocent that you don't realize making love is very natural. Very pleasurable." His voice was quiet, calm. He was attempting to reassure her. "You will see there is no reason for fear, or shame."

She stared across the tent at the off-white canvas walls with the flickering shadows cast by the candlelight. But she was fearful, and ashamed.

In America or England what happened to her was called rape. In America or England there might have been justice. But in Baraka…

In Baraka she'd be blamed. In Baraka she would have been held accountable. Punished. A virtuous girl wouldn't be where she wasn't supposed to be. A virtuous girl remained hidden, private, protected.

But Keira, ever adventurous, the half-English teenager with a liberal mother, had thought herself exempt from Barakan laws.

And she'd paid. She'd paid for her innocence and foolishness, she'd paid for her boldness and daring. She'd paid in spades.

"Trust me," he said. "Everything will be fine."

Trust him? Her stomach did a funny somersault. If only it were so easy.

The festivities ended late, and by the time Kalen and Keira returned to her tent, she was drooping with fatigue.

Kalen held the tent flap open for her. "Take your time," he said. "Change. Make yourself comfortable. There's no hurry."

Keira didn't need a lot of time to change. One of the robed Berber women helped her undress and Keira slipped immediately into her nightgown before crawling exhausted into bed. She tried to stay awake, waiting for Kalen, but her eyes were too heavy.

Surely if she fell asleep, he'd leave her alone, wouldn't he?

Surely he wouldn't force himself on her tonight?

Keira was woken by the unexpected shift of the mattress beneath her. Suddenly there was warmth beside her where previously there'd been none.

Arms reached for her, pulled her against a bare chest. Keira stiffened in protest. "Relax," Kalen's voice whispered in her ear. "Nothing's going to happen. Go back to sleep."

But she wasn't sleepy anymore. She felt violently awake, panic zinging through her veins, adrenaline making every thought razor sharp and clear.

She didn't like being held so closely.

She didn't like the feel of his naked body against her.

She didn't like the surprise or her sense of powerlessness.

"I can't see," she choked. "Turn on the light."

"There's nothing to see. It's just you here, and me."

But her pulse still raced. Her nerves screamed, alarmed and she tried to push away.

Yet the harder she pushed at his arms, the closer he held her. "Please, Kalen, let me go."

"Keira, it's just me," he murmured, gently stroking her upper arm. "Relax. Nothing bad is going to happen."

"I can't do this tonight, Kalen, I can't—"

"You don't have to. We're not going to do anything. Just sleep."

"We're not having sex?"

"No."

"We're just going to sleep?"

"Yes."

She drew a short breath, heart still pounding. "You're sure?"

"Yes."

"Promise me, Kalen, promise me you won't touch me."

She felt his chest rise and fall with a deep sigh

of aggravation. "It's a good thing I'm learning to deflect your insults, *laeela*."

"But you have no clothes on."

"I know. And unfortunately, you do."

The panic still hovered there, humming in her mind like the frenzied wings of a dragonfly. "You have to wear something."

"Why?" His irritation seemed to give way to amusement.

"Because it's decent."

"There's nothing indecent about nudity."

She sniffed, tilting her face away from him. "I'm not comfortable."

"Then get comfortable because I always sleep naked," he answered and tugged her even more firmly against him, his muscular arms locking around her, his hands cupped over her abdomen. "And soon so will you."

The heat of his body penetrated her thin night-gown and the press of his hands on her stomach made her insides feel hot, molten, far from settled. "I seriously doubt it."

"I think we could do with a little more optimism."

"You might just want to get another wife."

He didn't laugh even though that's what she'd intended. Instead his arms tightened around her, holding her even more closely. "Not a chance in hell," his voice rasped in her ear.

For a long moment it was quiet in the tent, so dark and still she could hear them breathe.

Feel the steady beat of his heart. Absorb his body's warmth.

With his arms wrapped around her, her back pressed to his chest, her hips cradled by his, she felt the strangest confidence, the confidence of unity. Shared strength.

"Innocence isn't something to be ashamed of," Kalen said a few minutes later, his voice sounding like velvet in the darkness. "If anything, it's admirable. I admire you."

"For being a virgin."

"Yes."

She smiled in the dark, smiled because he thought he was helping and yet he was only making everything worse. "Why would you admire me more for being a virgin at twenty-three?"

"It shows respect and self-worth. Respect for your body, and self-worth because you haven't given yourself to the first man that asks."

"I suppose you could assume whatever you want. Men usually do."

His chest rose and fell with silent laughter. "Sexist?" he teased.

"And feminist."

"So tell me, how does a feminist become a Dallas Cowboy cheerleader?"

She hesitated a long moment, thinking of her radical mother, her conservative father, her life split between different countries, different cultures. "Very, very carefully."

He laughed again and Keira shifted in his arms, turning to face him, forgetting for a moment her own self-consciousness. "You know my mother was a die-hard feminist, don't you? One of England's finest radicals."

"I'd heard about her liberal background."

"Liberal is putting it mildly." Keira had never understood her mother. Never understood how intellectual theory could be more appealing than spending time with her own daughter. When her mother wasn't writing another of her many books on social evolution and the rise and fall of female power in the West, her mother was on the lecture circuit, the ever popular Dr. Gordon on university campuses in Europe and North America.

"Yet your father isn't liberal," Kalen said.

"But that was father's charm. Father was the ultimate challenge. And Mother could never resist a good challenge."

"You're angry with her."

"Not angry. She's dead." Killed by a cancer three years ago she didn't even know she had until it was too late to do anything but say shocked, hurried goodbyes.

Her mother, flinty tough with her amazing cerebral powers, felled by her own body, by a cancer unique to women.

Her mother, in one of her favorite speeches, said women were cursed by their uteruses. How ironic that she died from uterine cancer. Was fate laughing? Crying?

"You miss her."

"I do. But even if she were alive today, we wouldn't be close." Keira's lips tugged but the smile wouldn't come. "I wasn't enough of a challenge for her."

"You're nothing but a challenge, *laeela*."

"No. I was a product of her womb, not her mind. Now Mother's students…those she loved. Her students adored her. Her readers embraced every word that came from her pen. I just wanted to play dolls and make sticky toffee custards."

He kissed her forehead, his lips tender against her skin. "I love sticky toffee custards."

Keira laughed and then reached up to swipe at dry eyes. "I can't imagine you eating puddings."

"Maybe that's because there's a great deal you don't know about me." He kissed her again, this time on her lips before settling her into his arms.

She nestled against him, found a place for her

cheek against his chest, and wrapped in his arms, the sound of his heart beating beneath her ear, she fell asleep.

By the time she woke in the morning, Kalen was gone and yet she still felt warm, and very relaxed.

She'd slept well for the first time in weeks.

For a few minutes she lay snugly beneath the covers, in no hurry to get up. Instead she let herself waken slowly, her body so relaxed she didn't think she'd ever move again.

Had she slept all night in Kalen's arms? She couldn't imagine it, but she also couldn't explain her unusual sense of peace.

The peaceful sensation was soon interrupted by shouts and banging noises outside the tent.

Rising regretfully, Keira pulled a robe over her nightgown and stuck her head outside the tent to see what was going on.

Men were moving quickly through the camp. The tents were coming down. The canvas shelters were swiftly rolled and tied into stiff bundles while at the edge of camp the camel drivers were shouting, *"Utsh! Utsh!"* at the camels, trying to get the huge animals to their knees to load them with the packed boxes and bags.

One of the animals—not hers, thank goodness—was roaring in protest as the first of the saddlebags was tied to his back. With every additional item he roared fresh protest, baring his teeth, spitting furiously, forcing the camel driver to dance back and forth to avoid being bitten.

Kalen had been standing with a group of men and someone must have said something because he turned, saw her, and long white robes flapping, he headed her way.

"*Sbah l-khir.*" Good morning, he said, his golden gaze speculative as he leaned forward to touch his lips to her right cheek and her left.

It was a public greeting, and even before his lips brushed her cheek, she felt her stomach somersaulting.

But the moment his mouth touched her skin, she sighed, lashes dropping, her whole body tingling with pleasure.

She remembered the night in his arms...

Remembered the feel of his chest against her own...

Remembered the way his legs slipped between hers, keeping her secure in his embrace...

"Did you sleep okay?" she asked, trying to disguise the crazy effect he was having on her.

From the faint smile playing at his gorgeous lips she didn't think she'd done a very good job disguising anything. "Very well," he answered, golden eyes sparking with amusement and something else. "And you?"

"Good."

His smile accented the deep grooves at the corner of his lips and she stared fascinated at his mouth, at the fullness of the lower lip. Had he kissed her last night? She could have sworn she felt his mouth against her neck, his lips traveling lightly across her collarbone.

"I didn't disturb your sleep?" she asked faintly, half remembering a hand stroking her hip, the indentation of her waist...

"No," he answered. "Did I disturb yours?"

She seemed to remember a hand measuring her ribs...

A warm palm cupping her breasts...

The same palm rubbing teasingly across her nipples, her nipples hardening, her body arching in sweet aching protest...

She frowned, brows knitting together. She looked away, telling herself it didn't happen. "No."

"Good. You needed a good night's sleep."

His words said one thing, his tone another, and she glanced up at him, saw laughter in his warm golden gaze, and blatant hunger, too.

He wanted her. He wanted her more now than he'd ever wanted her and she shivered in the face of such raw desire.

Kalen had changed, she thought, unable to look away from the hunger and possession in his eyes.

In London he'd exuded an air of mystery and detachment, a bored cynicism that suited his title and wealth. But this morning, with the sun burnishing his black hair, the blue sky still, the temperature quickly climbing, Kalen was anything but detached.

His emotions weren't cloaked, either. Everything about him seemed immediate. Accessible. His hunger. His desire. The whisper of dark, intense passions.

The sheikh had returned to the desert, and the desert with its sun and wind and sea of sand had brought the sheikh to life.

"You'll want to dress," he said, as two men staggering beneath the weight of wooden crates stumbled past. "Your breakfast is waiting. We'll be leaving within a half hour."

"Where are we going?"

"To my kasbah in Ouaha, and the rest of the camp is moving on."

"And my father?"

"He's going back to Atiq." Kalen smiled warmly, indulgently down at her. "I don't think he's comfortable enough with me yet to join us on our honeymoon."

CHAPTER TEN

HONEYMOON. Keira carefully said the word; let it sit in her mouth, on her tongue, as she dressed.

Honeymoon. She felt an insidious curl of heat in her belly and felt again that hard, warm palm cupping her breast, applying tormenting pressure to a sensitized nipple...

Sooner or later Kalen would want to consummate their relationship. It's what honeymoons traditionally represented, but she shied away from completing the picture.

She was incredibly attracted to Kalen, but she was also scared. She didn't know enough. He knew too much.

She forced herself to finish dressing and then eat some of the breakfast prepared—a pita filled with saffron, scrambled egg and onion—before they set off, a camel caravan, departing the way Kalen and his men had arrived.

It was a long day, and they stopped only briefly for a hasty lunch. When Keira got hungry, Kalen offered her a bag of sweet, plump dates for her to snack on. "Dates are a perfect food for the desert," he said. "They provide salt, water, sugar and vitamins."

Later, with the sun drilling overhead, mirages shimmering in the distance, Keira felt lulled by the rocking motion of the camels, the subtle tints and shadows of the desert, the peculiar sense that time had stopped and the rest of the world had fallen away.

Her dreamy state was abruptly broken when one of Kalen's men drew up alongside him to speak quietly but urgently. Kalen listened attentively; nodded, said a few words and the man rode off.

This happened three more times in the next several hours.

Something, Keira thought, studying Kalen's profile, was up. And while Kalen's outward expression appeared calm, unruffled, she sensed a new alertness about him. A readiness.

For what?

Were they being watched? Followed? Was Abizhaid giving pursuit?

She'd half expected retaliation from Ahmed Abizhaid. Kalen had stolen her out from under his nose, paid triple the bride price, married her in front of everyone last night…

Ahmed Abizhaid couldn't be happy…

But Kalen didn't mention anything to her, expressed neither concern nor fear, and late in the day they finally stopped, setting up camp in the *wadi,* or seasonal riverbed.

As they'd traveled that day the terrain had gradually begun to change. They were still surrounded by sand, but red rocky mountain peaks shaded the horizon, and warped, gnarled trees broke the stark dunes of sand.

Kalen's party consisted of maybe twenty men, half were the Sultan's guards from Atiq, and the rest a mixture of Berbers, their tribes identifiable by the various robes and head covers worn. But each man had a job as they set up camp, including the cook who prepared a traditional Barakan dinner of lamb stew to be scooped with warm chewy bread.

During dinner someone came to the tent entrance, announced himself and was immediately summoned forward by Kalen.

Kalen rose, clasped the man's hand and they kissed, once on each cheek.

Kalen greeted him as though he were an equal, and without introducing him to Keira the two moved off, crouching down together, they began to talk long and earnestly.

The stranger was also bringing news, Keira thought, and Kalen's expression grew more and more somber.

As the men continued to talk, Keira studied the white robed stranger with the fierce dark eyes. He was tall, well built, his hard features sun-burnt and yet there was an untamed element about him, as if he was more warrior than man.

He wasn't one of the men traveling with Kalen, and he wasn't one of the Sultan's guards, either. He was a Berber, she knew that much. He wore his hair relatively long, an inky-black combed back from his broad brow and fierce eyes. So who was he, and what was his relationship with Kalen?

As she chewed on the doughy *m'lla,* bread of the sands, she tried to catch some of the conversation exchanged between Kalen and the stranger but the few words she managed to overhear weren't Arabic, at least not the Arabic she'd learned in school.

Then abruptly the stranger stood, left and Kalen rejoined her.

"I have to go," Kalen said. "My guest has traveled a great distance. We have much to discuss."

She was right. The stranger had only just arrived. "Who is he? I don't recognize him."

"Sheikh Tair. A Berber chieftain from neighboring Ouaha. An old friend."

So it was Berber they were speaking then, or at least, a Berber dialect. "He looks quite...fierce."

"The Berbers are famous warriors." He stooped down, kissed her on the forehead and then rose again, his powerful body curiously graceful. "But they're also known for their warmth and hospitality." He turned away, prepared to leave.

"Kalen." Her voice stopped him. He looked over his shoulder at her. "You are strategizing," she said softly. "I know you. And your men. They bring you reports, don't they?"

The black lashes fringing his eyes narrowed. His features firmed. "You're not in any danger. I promise."

She got to her feet, closed the distance between them. "I'm not worried about me," she answered, and it was true. She felt safe here in the desert. Safe and calm. But Kalen she worried about. "Are *you* in danger?"

He reached out to run a finger through the tendril of hair lying on her shoulder. "There are always risks, *laeela,* but these are calculated. And the men with me, they are the best of the tribesmen."

"You will fight Sidi Abizhaid, won't you?"

He pressed the inky tendril back against her shoulder, traced the silk strand down, over her breast. "Not today."

Then he lifted her chin, kissed her lips, and left.

Keira couldn't sleep. She lay in the low bed on the floor of the tent, sheets and covers thrown back, a pillow bunched beneath her cheek.

It had been hours since Kalen had left. She'd even stepped outside the tent earlier to see if she could spot him but he was nowhere in sight, and the other tents were dark, quiet.

There were men posted outside her tent, though, their faces shrouded, wrapped in dark blue fabric leaving just their eyes visible.

Berbers, she thought, knowing that historically the Berbers were nomadic and warlike, their culture as mystical as it was mysterious.

She wondered at Kalen's close association with the tribes. In many ways he seemed more comfortable with the tribesmen than he did with Atiq's urban sophistication.

"Sheikh Nuri?" she asked the sentry closest to her. The man shook his head, and gesturing, indicated he wanted her to return to her tent.

As he lifted his arm, she noticed the sword in his robe's belt, and the leather holster slung beneath his arm.

He was heavily armed. Interesting.

She returned to her tent and climbed into bed, and waited for Kalen. And as she waited, she forced herself to confront truths she hadn't been willing to admit in years.

She loved Baraka.

She loved the Barakan part of her.

And yet all these years she'd kept her distance, all

these years she'd tried to erase her father's culture from her. But despite the seven years in England and America, she'd never successfully gotten the exotic rhythm of Baraka from her blood.

In Dallas, when she used to look in a mirror she always saw the dark blue desert sky in her eyes, and the history of the people in her black hair. She might want to be English—might want to think like an American—but she'd known deep in her heart that she was still half Barakan, still half desert, half heat, half endless sun.

Truthfully she was glad to be back, glad to make peace with this part of her past.

Hours passed but Kalen didn't return. Keira fought to stay awake but eventually she gave up the battle, and gave in to sleep, with her final thought being, Kalen should be here...

And he was there when she woke at dawn. He slept close to her, facing her, one of his long, muscular arms stretched out above her head.

He was naked, as far as she could tell, his dark hair tousled, his skin a gleaming gold.

But it was his warmth she found most seductive.

His warmth seemed to penetrate the sheets, the cover, her skin itself.

She rolled over onto her stomach to better study

his face. She liked him asleep. His hard jaw was not quite so angular. His long nose less regal.

Instead he just looked like a man. A very, very handsome man.

In her bed. The corner of her mouth tilted. Gently she reached out, touched the short black strands of hair hanging over his brow, and then very, very lightly, the elegant sweep of his prominent cheekbone. His jaw was shadowed with a day's growth of beard and his lips, slightly parted, looked incredibly appealing against the black stubble of his beard.

She kissed him lightly, so lightly he didn't stir. Bittersweet emotion welled up. Sheikh Kalen Nuri. Dream. Fantasy.

Not to mention aggressive desert chieftain.

Carefully, as not to disturb him, she slid back beneath the covers, crept closer to his warmth and let her body curve into his, savoring his heat, his strength, and the rare pleasure of feeling not just peace, but a hint of sweet contentment. It was a good feeling, she thought, one she could definitely get used to.

She didn't know at what point he reached for her, but she stirred as his hand slid across her midriff, a slow lazy exploration that made waking a delicious pleasure.

Keira held her breath as his palm slid up, over

her ribs to brush the underside of her breasts and then down again, a long leisurely stroke over her now tense belly. For long minutes he just touched her—and she lay still, barely daring to breathe.

It felt lovely being touched this way, not at all frightening, nothing aggressive.

She let herself concentrate on the stirring of the senses, the seductiveness of being caressed. His hand was so warm through the thin cotton of her nightgown and as he stroked the length of her abdomen and around her hip, she arched, trying to get closer to him, wanting to feel more of his warmth, some of his skin.

As she arched, he shifted her, turning her to face him, settling her securely in the crook of his arm.

His lips brushed her cheek, lightly, so lightly she felt her lashes drift closed. His mouth moved across her other cheek, a drifting kiss that stirred the nerves, made her skin heat, her body grow hotter, more pliant still.

She pressed closer, felt one of his knees move between hers, felt his hand trail down her back.

His mouth had felt so good against hers and she leaned against his chest, trying to recapture the pleasure. He let her stretch, let her struggle a moment before he rewarded her effort with a kiss. There was more pressure in his lips this time, and her mouth quivered beneath his, lips parting, breath escaping.

The kiss wasn't enough, the pressure still too fleeting. She sank her fingers into his chest, felt the firm dense muscle of his body beneath her frantic touch.

Her mouth chased his, her lips holding his, her lips asking—demanding—to be satisfied. She wanted more from his mouth, more strength, more hunger, more passion.

The scrape of his teeth. The caress of his tongue. The softness of his inner lip. The smoothness of the inside of his cheek. She wanted it all. The textures, the sensations, the experience.

He rolled onto his back and drew her on top of him. She had to lean forward, prop herself on one elbow to kiss him better. His mouth felt even sexier like this. She could control the pressure, the intensity, the pace, slipping her tongue into his mouth, sliding the tip along his upper lip, feeling his hoarse breath as she struck a sensitive nerve.

With one hand she touched his cheek, the rough bristles of his beard against her palm as she kissed him more deeply, driven somehow to connect with him, to close that distance between them. She'd been so lonely for so long and to be like this with him, to feel so safe, so wonderful…

He gave himself to her, meeting her demands,

answering her feverish kiss with a dark passion of his own.

Tension coiled in her belly as his tongue stroked hers, as his hands caressed the length of her. She felt all stirred, all jittery, and yet she wasn't sure what to do next.

He felt her tremble and he drew an arm all the way around her body, holding her fast, keeping her locked to his chest, his hips, his legs.

The heat and hardness of his body penetrated her nightgown. The thin barrier was almost a distraction, a barrier, one more thing between her and Kalen. But she tried to block it out, tried to focus on satisfying her terrible hunger.

She wanted him. Needed him. Needed to push him somehow, to find what it was in him she'd wanted so badly, that she'd craved all these years.

He'd been a drug and she'd been an addict. She'd wanted him so badly, she'd wanted to be close, to be held closely, very closely, held as though she were the only woman for him.

But she didn't know how to seduce him, didn't know how to be more aggressive. While she wanted him, she was also uncertain about her skills...her finesse.

Someone like Kalen had been with so many women, had enjoyed women with confidence and experience, women practiced in the art of seduction.

She couldn't give him practiced moves, couldn't give him worldly sophistication. She could only give him her. Give him her heart, her love, her loyalty.

She prayed it would be enough.

He stroked the length of her back, his hand settling in the small of her spine, and then slipping lower, caressing the curve of her hip, the roundness of her bottom. It felt as if he were lighting sparklers beneath her skin. Her body grew hotter, her nerves tauter, more electric.

She shuddered as he continued to caress her bottom, tempted to part her legs, tempted to give him access to her most private self but fear held her back.

She couldn't bear to be hurt again...especially not by him.

But he didn't push her, didn't rush her and as he caressed her the aching sensation in her belly spread. Her womb felt unbearably heavy. She felt embarrassingly wet between her thighs. She was so turned on, knew she wasn't the only one turned on. He'd been hard for ages, she'd felt the press of his arousal against her thigh, but also felt his control. He was holding back, restraining himself for her sake.

She didn't know what to do next, didn't know how to proceed to the next step. If only she knew it wouldn't hurt—that he wouldn't hurt her—but there were no guarantees and helplessly she kissed him again, offering him the only thing she knew how.

He touched her face, fingertips tracing her brow bone and then her cheek. "Are you scared?" he murmured against her brow.

"Yes."

"What scares you?"

"Pain."

"I'll do my best not to hurt you."

She wanted to believe him. She did. And his touch was so gentle, so loving, it caught her heart, squeezed it tight.

"I want to touch you," he said, "and if anything hurts, or scares you, tell me to stop. And I will. I promise."

If anything hurts, or scares you...

She wrapped an arm around Kalen's neck, holding on for dear life. She was trembling, but now with fear. "Okay."

He kissed her again, kissed her deeply, his tongue exploring the inside of her lips, the cheek of her mouth, the edge of her teeth. And as he kissed her, she felt him reach between her legs, slowly, very slowly. He was parting her thighs, making room for his hand.

His fingertips brushed the curls between her thighs. She felt moisture on her skin, her moisture. She went hot all over.

He was brushing her curls again, and then gently, lightly, slipping fingertips across her softness that was slick and hot.

She gasped, dug her fingers into his shoulders. His touch felt wonderful. It wasn't frightening, it was sexy, teasing. He stroked her so lightly, making her feel so much in so many different places. She ached for him deep inside her body. She felt a terrible tension on the outside. When he stroked across her clitoris it was like heaven and earth coming together—a riot of sensation, so much sensation she didn't know whether to squeeze her legs together or beg him to put his finger inside her.

And then he did slip a finger inside her, and she froze. It was a helpless fear, perhaps a fear of the unknown more than anything because his touch was so pleasurable and yet she feared rejection, his rejection.

What if he didn't like this, the way she responded? What if he didn't like *her?*

"What's wrong?" he murmured against her mouth. "Did I hurt you?"

"No." Hot emotion filled her chest. He read her so easily, understood her almost too well.

"Does this feel okay?" He was slowly sliding his finger in and then out.

She felt her muscles tighten around him, tighten for him. "Yes."

"What else would you like?"

She shook her head, unable to answer.

"Tell me, *laeela*. I won't know how to please you if you don't tell me."

"But you are pleasing me. It's me. I'm afraid of disappointing you."

His chest lifted, fell. He'd taken a great breath. "Never." His voice came out rough. "Never. I swear."

His free hand reached up to cup the back of her head, urging her head down again, holding her mouth more firmly to his. He'd allowed her to kiss him earlier, but now he took the lead, and he kissed her deeply, even as he touched her intimately, stirring her, creating a fierce need.

His kiss and touch held magic, the sorcery of talent, practice, expertise. And with that magic, he drew from her a response that stunned her. She felt as if her grip on reality was receding, felt as if there were different worlds out there, worlds she'd never known. Her body was no longer controlled or contained but danced in his hands, alive, dangerous, explosive.

If he didn't stop touching her soon, she'd fall apart in his hands.

She wanted to give to him. She wanted to open for him. She wanted to belong to him in every sense of the word.

"Take my nightgown off," she whispered against his mouth, maddened by the fabric tangling between her legs, the nightgown keeping her from being feeling Kalen against her.

"Sit up."

She did, her thighs parted, straddling his hips, her damp, sensitized core pressed to the length of his erection. She ought to be embarrassed but she wasn't. She actually wanted more, seduced by his touch, seduced by the pleasure.

He tugged the hem of her nightgown up, up over her head and discarded it by the side of the bed.

And then his hands were on her skin, her bare skin that felt so hot and sensitive.

Adroitly he rolled over, holding her hips securely, and now she was beneath him, her thighs spread, his warm body pressing against her, his erection rubbing against her dampness.

As his rigid shaft slid up and down against her wet softness, he nearly slipped inside and she gasped, tensing.

"If it hurts, say stop," he whispered, reminding her of their agreement.

She nodded and he lowered his head, kissed her deeply, his kiss distracting her, calming her, and as she relaxed she felt him press against her.

No pain yet and she drew a breath.

She felt the silken tip of his shaft enter her. Instinct made her want to protest, but his kiss drugged her, his kiss intense, sensual, demanding. He reached between them, stroked her tummy, and then up to cup her breast. He rolled her nipple between his finger and thumb and the riot of different sensations made it impossible to focus on any one thing. Instead she felt mindless, heavy with wanting, and the pressure of him inside her wasn't pain... just different...just a hot stretching sensation...a fullness.

It's not pain, she reminded herself as he pushed deeper, it's just Kalen, it's just Kalen making love to you. But part of her mind still wanted to protest. Part of her wanted to shut off, pull away, but she reached up to circle his nape, run her fingers through his hair, stay focused on touching him. Kalen. Her Kalen.

He was moving, slowly, smoothly, pulling out and then slowly, smoothly he entered her again. This time there was less pressure, the sensation of being stretched was less strong. He continued to enter her only to gradually withdraw until the feeling became pleasing, no, more than pleasing, infinitely satisfying.

It was good holding him so close, his body buried in hers warmed her all the way through. Her skin glowed. Her nerves felt tight. Her senses keenly awake.

"Kalen," she whispered his name, her voice pitched low, husky with desire. Her arms wound more closely around his neck. His chest scraped her breasts. She couldn't believe how good he felt, couldn't believe how comfortable she felt.

"Should I stop?" he asked, kissing her, sucking her tongue into his mouth.

His kiss nearly put her over the edge. She shuddered against him, and as she shuddered, he dipped his tongue into her mouth and drove deeper with his hips. The combination of his hot, hard erection inside her body and his cool, slick tongue in her mouth was so erotic, so exciting she whimpered, absolutely wanton. She wanted more. It felt so good, being with him felt so good. *Too good.*

The sun outside was just beginning to rise, painting broad yellow and pink streaks against the canvas, much like the warmth he was creating in her.

Pulse quickening, Keira lifted her hips to take him deeper, sucked on his tongue to keep his cool wetness in her mouth. And every thrust was a deliberate seduction of the senses. Her skin felt so hot and sensitive. Her nerves were getting wound so tight. She pressed her knuckles to his back, clung to him, her breath increasingly shallow.

He was doing this to her, she thought, heat engulfing her, his body driving her toward a sizzling warmth, an explosive pleasure.

"Kalen," she choked against his mouth feeling positively frantic.

But he didn't stop moving, just pressed deeper, and then withdrew almost completely only to bury his shaft in her as though her body had been made for him, and maybe it had because she couldn't imagine anything ever feeling better than this…

As the pleasure overwhelmed her, her body began tightening, muscles deep inside her clenching, trying to hold Kalen. Suddenly she was shattering, a hot dazzling explosion through time and space. She cried out, against his mouth, and his kiss took her cry of pleasure into him.

Shuddering in his arms, she felt wave after wave of sensation ripple over her, through her, the sensation so strong she couldn't escape. And then he was shattering, too, burying himself in her in a fierce orgasm.

She was still clinging to him, heart pounding,

skin flushed and damp when a voice shouted outside the tent.

"Your Excellency!" the man cried. "A caravan approaches. Sheikh Tair goes out to meet them."

Kalen kissed her swiftly and immediately rolled out of bed, grabbing clothes and climbing into them as he headed out.

Keira dressed quickly as well. Within minutes of Kalen exiting the tent, the whole encampment had come to life. Tents came down, men packed crates and leather satchels. Camel drivers strapped the boxes and bags to the camels' backs.

By the time Kalen reappeared, their tent had been packed up, their bed torn apart and put away, the pillows and covers tied in bundles.

"Are we in danger?" she asked, as Kalen took her hand, led her to her kneeling camel.

"No. Tair has many men between us and the caravan—"

"It's Sidi Abizhaid, isn't it?"

"Mmmm. It's wise if we get moving, try to cross the border into Ouaha. No one likes to be a sitting duck." He assisted her onto the camel's back and then leaned forward, kissed her on each cheek, murmuring as he did so, "I'm sorry we were interrupted."

She blushed. "National security always comes first, Your Excellency."

He smiled, white teeth flashing, eyes gold like the sun-kissed sands. "I hope we can continue later… if you're not too sore."

She blushed again, incredibly self-conscious as hot bands of color burned her cheekbones. "I am fine."

His hand covered hers. "I didn't hurt you?"

Hurt her? He'd been the most unbelievable lover. She'd been kissed, touched, pleasured beyond her wildest expectations. *"No."*

"And I didn't scare you?"

"No." She couldn't hide the sparkle in her eye. "Not at all."

"Good." He squeezed her hands gently then stepped away. "Remember, *laeela,* I am always close by."

As they traveled that day the red sand gave way to red rocks, and the slope of sand dunes became steep hills.

In the distance there were scattered groves of trees, little oases of green in all the beige, pink and red.

This morning had to mean something, she thought, glancing at Kalen as they rode toward the red city in the distance. The lovemaking had been so incredible it had felt…sacred.

Was making love this intense, this physical, and this sensual for everyone?

Her body had felt beautiful in his hands. *She'd* felt beautiful. Everything about being together had felt so right.

Kalen drew his camel alongside Keira's. "We've just crossed the border," he said. "We've left Baraka, have entered Ouaha. We should reach my kasbah in another couple of hours. But first we'll pass through Zefrou, an old Berber town. In Zefrou we'll stop, have tea."

"You're not worried about Sidi Abizhaid anymore?"

"This is Sheikh Tair's jurisdiction."

"What does that mean?"

"If Abizhaid commits a crime here, I cannot touch him. Abizhaid becomes Sheikh Tair's responsibility."

She shot Kalen a swift, assessing glance. "But Sheikh Tair is your friend."

Kalen's eyes gleamed. "Indeed."

"Is that…fair?"

"Is it fair that Abizhaid raids border towns to finance his coalition of rebels and malcontents? Or that Tair's wife and young son were killed in cold blood in one of the attacks a year ago?"

He saw the shock in her eyes and nodded. "Abizhaid is a soulless outlaw. A thug, a thief, he takes what he wants from who he wants and cuts the throats of those who stand in his way."

Kalen's words filled her with fear, a black name-less, formless fear that couldn't be described. "And my father?" she asked, looking away, staring numbly at the red mountains rising in the distance.

"He's in danger."

"But he's not the danger."

"No. Abizhaid manipulates your father, makes him obey by intimidation."

"And yet my father was going to force me to marry him."

"Abizhaid had said he'd kill you if Omar didn't arrange the marriage."

CHAPTER ELEVEN

KEIRA'S head whipped around so hard she nearly lost her balance. Groping for the bar on the camel's back that served as a pommel, she clung tightly, clung for all she was worth. "Who told you that?"

"Your father. The night we were married."

"Then why did Father triple the bride price? Why did he throw opposition in the way?"

"He was bluffing. Trying to appear loyal to Abizhaid knowing that Abizhaid has spies everywhere. Yet later, your father refused to accept a penny of the *sedaq*. He's grateful you're in my protection. But it doesn't lessen the threat on his head."

She shook her head, not knowing what to believe. "So why didn't Father ever go to the Sultan? Why didn't he ask for the Sultan's help?"

"Because your father has been blackmailed by Abizhaid for nearly a decade."

"Blackmailed for what?"

"Years ago your father shared information once

with a woman—a woman he loved, and believed loved him—that resulted in an attempt on the Sultan's life. Malik nearly died."

Keira's stomach churned. "Who was the woman?"

"One of Abizhaid's wives."

Keira gripped the handle tighter. "You know this?"

"I'd long suspected, but your father confirmed everything yesterday. We spoke for a long time. He's relieved it's over, Keira. He's been living with this tremendous burden for years."

"He's going to help you then?"

"He's offered to testify against Abizhaid—"

She drew a slow breath, understanding the implications of publicly denouncing a powerful warlord like Ahmed Abizhaid. "It'll get him killed for certain."

"Your father understands the risks. But the rewards outnumber the risks. Abizhaid will pay for his crimes. The Sultan and people of Baraka and Ouaha will be safer. Your father might even have a chance at a normal life, one lived without so much guilt and fear."

A life lived without guilt and fear…she felt a stirring of envy. She'd love such a life, too. "What will happen to Father after he testifies? Will he have to go to jail?"

"There might be prison time. Or knowing Malik, my brother might also choose to pardon your father. But first, Abizhaid has to be captured. And that's what Sheikh Tair has agreed to help me do."

A rider on horseback appeared on the horizon, haloed by the intense sun. The horse was traveling so fast it appeared to be flying through the sand, its hooves barely touching the ground.

Kalen watched the horse and rider for a moment, eyes narrowed. "Not good," he said quietly with a slow shake of his head. "This isn't going to be good news."

She looked at the horse and rider quickly gaining ground and then at Kalen whose features were now tightly drawn. "Who is it?"

"One of Tair's men." Kalen leaned forward on his camel, his shoulders briefly slumping. "Something's happened."

Kalen was right. The rider on horseback brought news of a surprise ambush. A number of Tair's men were killed, the sheikh himself was wounded.

"And Abizhaid?" Kalen asked, his gaze riveted on the young Berber's face.

"It was uncertain when I left, but it appears he escaped."

Kalen abruptly switched from Arabic to Berber, speaking quickly. The young man nodded. Kalen spoke again and with a last nod, the young man wheeled his horse around and took off, not in the direction he'd come, but toward the town of Zefrou, whose walls were just barely visible in the distance.

"He's gone to get a doctor," Kalen said, as the young man rode on.

"You're not going to help Sheikh Tair? I thought he was your friend—"

"Of course he's my friend. He and I go back many, many years. But you are my wife, and I will not leave your side until you're safe within the walls of my kasbah."

A half hour later the walls of Zefrou loomed large and Keira sat taller. From her first glimpse of the reddish mud walls, to the camels lounging beneath fragrant orange trees weighted with fruit, she suspected that little had changed here in the past thousand years.

The wood and mud brick town was scarred by centuries of sun, wind and rain. Zefrou's streets were filled not with cars but donkeys and oxen, and men and women alike were shrouded by hooded *jellabas*.

They stopped for tea at what appeared to be an impressive and yet crumbling house crafted from the same red mud as the rest of the town, but the inner house was a surprise. While the exterior looked old, almost decrepit, the heart of the house evoked old Moorish elegance and luxury. The bright, sun-lit reception rooms were detailed with stucco and intricate mosaic tiles and the thick mud walls washed with pink and ochre paint kept the rooms comfortably cool.

This trip had been a discovery, Keira thought, bowing deeply to her hosts, a man and woman greatly honored by Sheikh Nuri's visit. For the first time she realized that life in the countries that bordered the Mediterranean Sea—countries like Baraka, Morocco and Ouaha—wasn't just the congested city streets of Atiq or Tangiers with its noisy souks, throngs of tourists and strong European influence. Life was also the ancient rhythms of the interior, the treacherous roads, the exhausting distances between towns, and silence. The silence of the sands, the silence of the red mud kasbahs, the silence of the Berber people themselves.

Tea was usually a soothing ritual, and one the Berbers were proud of, but today Keira felt Kalen's impatience with the ceremony, his muscular body shifting restlessly. He was anxious. He wanted to be traveling. She knew that he wanted to see her settled in his fortified castle so he could be lending assistance to Tair.

But she couldn't suggest they leave. It was Kalen's decision. And Kalen was determined to conclude the tea service respectfully.

He was just beginning to give his thanks when a door in the house banged open and the sound of running feet and laughter echoed down the hallway.

Suddenly two girls burst into the room, their *jellabas* flying, hoods falling backward revealing long dark hair.

And then they realized what they had done. Interrupted the sheikh. During tea.

The girls grabbed at each other, horrified. Bowing, they immediately began to creep backward, trying to escape as fast as possible and yet before disappearing around the corner, one of the girls lifted her head and looked at Kalen for a lingering moment, her beautiful dark almond-shaped eyes ringed with kohl, her expression blatantly curious. Blatantly impressed.

Her father noticed. "Be gone!" he snapped, with a rough gesture of his hand.

The girl dropped her gaze but not before Keira saw the teenage girl's shy, dazzled smile.

Keira looked at Kalen. But Kalen wasn't looking at the girl anymore. He was looking at her. "She reminds me of you," he said softly, briefly touching her arm. "You used to look like that. Big eyes. Endless curiosity."

He was right, she thought, her arm tingling where he'd touched her. And she had been curious, so incredibly curious. But that was before she knew it was possible to fall so far from the state of grace, before she realized that one mistake would turn into a dozen more. Before she knew that certain injuries never healed but lasted, hurting when one least expected it. In the middle of the day. When confronted by perfect sunshine. At the end of a gorgeous piece of music. When a baby laughed.

"I made you sad," he said, touching her arm again, this time sliding down to clasp her hand, her palm pressed to his.

"No. Yes." And smiling she shook her head. "Don't worry."

"We should go then." He drew her to her feet. "It's getting late."

"You're worried about Sheikh Tair," she said softly as they left the cool dark house, returning to late-afternoon sunshine.

"There's been no word," he said.

"A bad sign?"

He hesitated. "An interesting one," he conceded.

Their camels were gone, replaced by horses. "We'll travel faster this way," Kalen explained. "We'll cut the time in half."

"So you are anxious about Tair?"

He circled her waist and easily lifted her into her saddle. "Curious, concerned, maybe. Anxious? No. The only thing I'm anxious about is that if we don't hurry, and I don't do what I need to do, I won't have enough time with you in bed."

"That's not important—"

"Not important? *Laeela,* this is our honeymoon."

She knew he was only half-serious, knew that beneath his jesting words and easy tone his thoughts were very much on the ambush that had taken place earlier in the day and getting aid to Tair and his men.

But Kalen would handle his worries his way, and he was determined to make Keira comfortable at his kasbah before leaving.

The sun was beginning to set by the time they reached his kasbah, and the clay fortress looked almost as red as the crimson sunset.

The kasbah was built nearly five hundred years ago high on the mountain, practically dug from the mountain, and yet it was more than just a fortress. It was like a city, completely walled, with carved turrets and towers, interior courtyards, fragrant gardens with sparkling pools.

Everything surprised and yet delighted. The doors were massive—huge studded wooden doors. The floors were paved with smooth pink flagstones. Doorways were arched. Windows on the lower floors were small, narrow, designed with safety in mind while the upper windows provided great expansive views.

The ancient mud kasbahs of the interior deteriorated rapidly in the intense dry heat but Kalen's kasbah had been lovingly maintained. Young palm trees shaded private gardens. A fountain gurgled outside Kalen's bedroom door. A large octagon pool shimmered beyond the fountain, the blue and white pool tiles reflecting the cloudless blue of the sky.

"This is…" she said, speechless as Kalen led her outside to the garden adjacent to his bedroom. "Unreal. A fantasy. Like something my father read to me from *Arabian Nights*."

"It is beautiful," he agreed, smiling faintly at her pleasure.

"But it's not a kasbah, Kalen. It's a palace. A palace fit for a sultan!"

"I know."

Her expression was humorous as she faced him. "You're not a sultan, are you?"

He shrugged. "Only in Ouaha."

Her jaw dropped, humor giving way to shock. "You're a sultan?"

"It's an honorary title more than anything."

She still wasn't thinking very fast but little things began to click into place. "That's why the couple who hosted us for tea were so in awe of you. And the teenage girls..."

"I consider myself a Berber chieftain like Tair, not a sultan, and speaking of Tair, I should go." He turned, his gaze skimming the pleasant garden with its fountain, palm trees and pool. "You'll be safe here. Well protected, I promise."

"I'm not worried."

"I could be gone a couple days."

"I understand."

He moved toward her, drew her into his arms and lifting her chin, kissed her. He kissed her deeply, thoroughly, kissed her until her head spun and her legs went weak. Kissed her until she reached for him, clinging to his robes, needing his strength to hold her up.

Finally he lifted his head. His amber gaze was dark, filled with rare emotion. "Stay inside the walls of the kasbah."

"I will."

"If anything goes wrong—"

"It won't." She stood up on tiptoe, kissed him on the mouth. "Do what you have to do. But come back soon."

He returned on the third day. The time had actually passed quickly for Keira. She'd immersed herself in kasbah life, joining the women in the kitchen, taking lessons in cooking some of the Berber specialties.

She was in the kitchen learning to bake a sweet honey, cinnamon and almond pastry when one of the serving girls shouted that Sheikh Nuri had been spotted, that he and his men should arrive in the next hour or so.

Keira tore her apron off, returned to her room and immediately began bathing, soaping up and down, washing her hair until it smelled of citrus and lavender.

After the bath, she applied a fragrant oil the women of the kasbah made, rubbing the oil into her still warm skin. The oil softened her skin, giving it a golden glow. She was just finishing rubbing the oil into her hands and feet when the bedroom door opened and Kalen stood there, tall, formidable, his gaze riveted on her.

"Don't move," he said, as she grabbed shyly for her bath towel.

"I'm naked," she protested, blushing profusely, her long dark hair still damp and clinging now to her oiled skin.

"I know." He shut the door behind him and deliberately locked it. "And I couldn't ask for a better welcome home."

She felt as if she were blushing all over. Her

skin felt so hot, so incredibly bare. "Let me finish dressing—"

"Absolutely not. You're beautiful. I want to look at you."

"*Kalen.*"

"Humor me, *laeela.* I've traveled a long way today just to return to you."

She bit her lip, flustered. "Sheikh Tair?" she asked, trying to distract him. "How is he?"

"In a hospital in Atiq. It's thought he'll recover completely."

"You must be relieved."

"I am," he answered steadily, but from the expression in his eyes she knew she hadn't distracted him yet. He was inspecting her, every bare inch of her.

"And Sidi Abizhaid?" she choked, feeling his gaze linger on her breasts and the dark hair curling at the junction of her thighs.

"Dead."

Her fingers itched to pick up her towel. "When? How?"

"He was killed in the ambush that wounded Tair. But because he'd disguised himself, no one immediately recognized him."

"What happens now?" she asked huskily, and there were really two meanings to the question. He knew it, too.

"Life goes on." He shrugged tiredly. "It has to. And I'd like nothing more than to forget the past seventy-two hours and just concentrate on you."

"On me?"

"Yes. Let me start with a bath. I'd love nothing more than a hot soak, and the company of my beautiful bride, and then…"

She blushed. "Let me start your bath." And before he could answer, she slipped into the ensuite bathroom with its high apricot colored mud walls and dark stenciling around the doorways and windows, knelt next to the hammered copper tub and turned the faucets on.

Her pulse raced but she wouldn't let herself think about anything but preparing the bath. She'd focus on one thing at a time, she told herself.

As the hot water filled the tub, Keira diligently crushed more of the herbs the women had given her for her bath—fragrant dried sprigs of lavender and rosemary—and dusted the crumbled herbs into the tub.

Aromatic scents wafted, mingling with the steam. She heard the bathroom door open. She didn't look up, aware that Kalen was watching her.

Aware that he wanted her and it was the strength of his desire that took her breath away. His passion stunned her, his passion fed her own.

Hand shaking slightly, she poured citrus scented

oil beneath the faucet, the oil made from the peel of oranges and lemons growing at the kasbah in one of the walled gardens.

He moved behind her, touched the top of her head. "You look like every man's fantasy come to life."

She bent her head. Her long hair swung forward, brushed her breast. "A slave girl from the Ottoman Empire?" she replied, blushing hotly.

He lifted her to her feet, turned her to face him. He held her firmly, his thighs trapping her bare legs between his own. "Hmmm. There's an interesting fantasy. It wasn't mine, but if you were my slave... what would I have you do for me?"

She couldn't help but look up, meet his eyes.

His amber gaze burned. He cocked his head, his black hair coated with a layer of sand and dust.

"Any ideas or suggestions, *laeela?*"

She felt so shy, so dreadfully inexperienced. "I could undress you."

"Yes."

"Bathe you."

"Bathe me?"

"You did say I was your slave girl."

He leaned her back against his arm, exposing her. With her long hair hanging loose, and her skin oiled and scented, she felt incredibly vulnerable. Soft, female, fragile.

Kalen's head dipped, his lips brushed her throat and then lower, to the swell of her breast. His lips closed around one nipple and he sucked it, softly and then harder.

She shuddered against him, hips writhing helplessly.

"Undress me," he said, lifting his mouth, stepping back.

She swayed on her feet. She felt completely disoriented. And then, heart pounding, hands shaking, she reached for his belt that secured his robe. Heat washed through her, heat and excitement.

She managed to get his belt loose. She dropped it on a low stool.

Glancing up into Kalen's face, she saw the fierce interest in his amber eyes. The fierceness of his desire jolted her. It was a physical thing, tangible, very much alive.

With an unsteady breath, she reached for his robe, tugged on the fabric, drew it from his shoulders, discarding the robe onto the stool along with the belt.

"Your pants," she said, mouth dry, heart hammering ferociously.

He sat down on the edge of the tub. She knelt at his feet, and keeping her eyes downcast, worked his trousers off, adding them to the pile of clothing.

She heard his soft laugh, a husky mocking sound

as he turned and slid into the bath. "So very shy," he taunted, sinking lower, and then groaning with pleasure as the hot water closed around him. "Heaven," he said, tilting his head back, resting it on the back of the tub.

For a moment she just drank him in with her eyes, letting herself have her fill.

With his dark hair, high bronze cheekbones, the full mouth with that lower lip of his that demanded kissing she wanted him, wanted to be with him again...

Leaning over, she placed a light kiss on the edge of his mouth. "I'll wash your hair. You keep your eyes closed and just relax."

Using a small silver bucket to wet his hair, she picked up the shampoo she'd used earlier and poured a generous amount into the palm of one hand.

Gently, firmly, she began to work the shampoo into his hair, massaging the liquid into a lather. She heard his soft hiss of pleasure as she rubbed the pads of her fingers deep against his scalp. She could see from his expression that he very much enjoyed the warm, steady pressure and she took her time, massaging the front hairline, the sides of his temple, the back of his head, the tension at his nape, around his ears. He sighed as she finished.

Shielding his eyes with one hand she rinsed the shampoo out.

"Now the rest of you," she said, picking up a sponge. Using the scented soap and the sponge she scrubbed his back, his broad shoulders, the sexy planes of his chest.

He lazily watched as she diligently washed his legs and feet. "The best slave girl I ever had."

Her eyebrows arched. "Thank you. I think." She sat back when she'd finished and handed him the soap. "I've done what I could. The rest is up to you."

"You've missed key spots."

"Deliberately." She knew she was blushing again. "Even slave girls have limits."

He laughed and taking the soap from her began to wash beneath the surface of the water.

Keira primly looked away, cheeks burning, her whole body equally hot and sensitive.

"You don't want to see my technique?" he teased, noting the prudish set of her lips and averted gaze.

"*No.*"

"You might learn something."

She cleared her throat. Lifted her chin. She wasn't even going to dignify that with a response.

And then suddenly she was being lifted, scooped

up off her knees, hauled by a wet sinewy arm over the edge of the tub and into the hot water itself.

"You might learn something," Kalen repeated lying back and settling her on him in the bathtub. She was soaked and shocked and gasping and he cupped her head in his hand, bringing her face down to his. "And you just might like it."

He covered her mouth in a searing kiss. He kissed her hard, a fierce kiss that consumed the senses, a kiss that was less about seduction than it was possession. The pressure of his mouth, the strength of his warm wet body, the rasp of hair on his chest against her breasts, the flat carved muscles of his abdomen against the softness of her belly made her head spin.

She couldn't think, couldn't seem to control anything, not when his lips were coaxing such a strong response, his tongue testing the seam of her lips, and then between her lips.

And she didn't know if it was the way he was kissing her, or the fact that she was naked and lying on him in the hot scented water, but she suddenly felt voracious, a woman desperate for a man. She wanted more from him, wanted to give him more of her.

As he kissed her, she slid her hands up his rib cage, across the width of his wide warm chest. The texture of his skin fascinated her, the satin surface

over hard, sleek, sinewy muscle; just as the texture of the damp, crisp hair between the plane of
chest muscle fascinated her, hair that tapered into
a narrow V down his chest, thinning at his belly
button. His nipples enticed her, the smallness, and
ending the kiss, she sank lower in the water, put
her mouth to his chest, lightly brushing his nipples
with her lips. She loved the silky feel of the small
nipples against her sensitive lip, the way he stiffened, groaned when she sucked on one and then
the other.

His body was big, beautiful, and she let him wrap
her in his arms, let his hands shape her against him,
let his warm delicious skin touch her, surround
her.

She didn't know what she was doing, and she
didn't care, and when Kalen flipped positions with
her in the tub, placing her beneath him only to
extend her arms and hold her hands above her head,
she let him.

She gasped when his head dropped and his mouth
brushed the swell of her breast. The warm water
lapped beneath her breast. His mouth pressed to
the side of her breast. The warmth was everywhere
and she felt liquid on the inside, melting for him.

She felt his hands on her thighs and then felt them
slide around to cradle her bottom as the tip of his
erection rubbed against her slit. She whimpered

at the maddening sensation, nerves teased but not satisfied. And then he was entering her and her lungs squeezed, her breath cut short. He was filling her, entering her deeply and it was a surprise, and while not painful, still startling.

That bodies could be joined so closely...

That people could become so intimate...

She shuddered as he began to move, burying his body in her, engaging her in this ancient dance. She felt everything and she wanted the feeling to last.

Her hands slid up his arms, fingers outlining the hard shape of muscle, the skin sleek and satin.

With him inside her, filling her, heating her, she felt the most intense welling of emotion. *I love you,* she wanted to tell him as he pushed her toward the brink, his body giving her the ultimate of pleasure. The words lingered in her mind, sitting in her heart, waiting on her tongue. *I love you, Kalen. Not because you need or want me to love you, because I can't help it. I don't know how not to love you.*

They ended up making love again a little later, this time on the bed, still half wrapped in bath towels, their scented oiled skin sliding smoothly against the other.

After the second climax, Keira couldn't move, warm and yet exhausted in Kalen's arms. "I know you need to eat," she whispered, eyes closed, body still floating. He'd shown her heaven and earth, she thought, given her a taste of bliss. "You've traveled far and now worked very hard..."

"Making love to you isn't work," he answered, combing through her long hair with his fingers. "I could make love to you all day."

The edge of her mouth lifted. "You'll definitely need nourishment for that."

"Maybe I'll just eat you—"

"Kalen!" Her head lifted. She frowned down at him. "No. Not a chance."

"Still so shy, *laeela*." He caressed the curve of her cheek with his thumb. "I've never met a woman as beautiful, or as bashful, as you."

"I'm not as shy as I was."

"No. But you've been a challenge." He brought her face down to his, pressed a long, lingering kiss to her lips. "I'm not complaining, though. I treasure the gift you gave me, that of your virginity. I am grateful you waited."

She began to grow cold as he talked, her body icing, muscles stiffening. "What if I wasn't a virgin?" she whispered, pulse unsteady. "What if I had had experience?"

"I suppose it'd depend on your definition of experience, but knowledge isn't a bad thing." He smoothed her hair back from her face, combing her hair over her shoulders and then down her back. "And yet the fact that you didn't have experience, made an impression on me. I was glad to be the first, glad I could teach you, love you, glad to be trusted with your innocence."

A wave of nausea hit. Nausea fueled by heartache. Heartache and guilt. She rolled out from beneath his arm, sat up on the edge of the bed. "I should see about your dinner."

"Keira." He leaned forward, grabbed her wrist, kept her from scooting off the bed. "Don't be ashamed of yourself. Everyone is different, everyone's emotions are different. I'm completely sincere when I say that I admire you. I respect the choices you've made—"

"But you don't know the choices I've made," she answered curtly, cutting him short. "You know so little about me, and my life."

He released her wrist, sat up, his body beautifully bare. "What don't I know?"

"Lots."

He shook his head. "I've known you since you were young, and I've had people look into you. Extensive investigations—"

"How far back did you go?"

His brow furrowed. "Quite far."

"Obviously not far enough then." There was a bite to her tone, anger in her words. He had to know the truth. She had to tell him. The guilt was eating her alive. But she also knew this wasn't the way to do it.

She should be calm, and she was far from calm at the moment.

But something was breaking apart inside of her, the protective barrier that had kept all the anger and shame locked safely inside her, and she felt driven to confess.

She'd never told anyone. But someone should know. Someone should know the truth, and she wanted that someone to be Kalen.

She needed Kalen to know her, want her for herself, not for some false notion he had about her and her sexual experience.

"I've something to tell you," she said stiffly. "It's important you know." She met his gaze, saw his puzzled expression, saw the warmth in his features began to fade.

She wanted to crawl back into his arms, wanted him to touch her again, hold her, because she was suddenly very afraid.

"Talk," he said bluntly. "You've got my full attention now."

CHAPTER TWELVE

SHE did, didn't she?

Gingerly Keira sat down again on the edge of the bed, her insides icy. "Something happened once, many years ago, and I thought…if I could be good, really good, I could fix everything. Fix me with goodness."

She leaned over, snagged one of the discarded bath towels and wrapped it around her. "I got near perfect marks in school. Danced every afternoon, an hour of barre followed by hours of rehearsal. I starved my body to get the look a ballerina needed. I did everything, absolutely everything asked of me. By everyone."

Keira shivered, and drew a slow breath, cold and confused, not by the truth, but by the number of years it took to reach this place.

She felt sorry for the girl hurt at the party, but also for the adult she'd become who could never get it right, who could never do enough.

But Kalen was silent, waiting for her to continue and she forced herself to go on. "I thought if I could just make everything all right for everyone else, I'd get lucky. I thought that God—fate—would look down from the sky and see me trying so hard. And God in all his compassion was going to reach down and save me. Give me another chance. Give me another life because I was good and I…"

The words were coming so fast she was shaking, trembling with tension and exhaustion. Seven years of silence, seven years of sorrow. "I deserved it.

"I deserved it," she repeated, looking briefly at Kalen, hands trembling in her lap. "I still do. And I want it. I want it with every bone in my body. I want forgiveness and compassion and most of all, hope."

But Kalen didn't say anything and her teeth had begun to chatter.

Her body burned, her body froze.

Everything was coming undone and it was like a great earthquake, the tearing apart of her defenses, the walls, the boundaries, the endless set of rules she'd given herself.

It was a death and a rebirth.

Karma. Fate. Change.

Shivering, she crossed her arms over her chest, over the semidamp towel. She'd spent her life trying to make up for a pain someone else had inflicted on her, lived to rid herself of a shame that had never made sense in the first place. Yes, she'd been in the wrong place but why did someone have to hurt her? And why did she have to be the one that couldn't have a good life, a rich, full life?

"I want a second chance," she concluded. "And perhaps you've given me that second chance but I need to hear it from you. I need to know you understand and you accept me the way I am."

"What did you do that was so bad?"

"I went to a party." She drew a breath for courage. "In Atiq. I was just a teenager."

Kalen's expression had grown increasingly guarded. The wariness in his eyes scared her. But she'd started this. She'd finish. "Things got carried away—"

"How?" he asked, lethally quietly.

"I had a drink, a cocktail. And…one thing led to another." She couldn't look at him anymore, not when he had such a peculiar expression on his face. Instead she kept talking, hoping he'd understand, hoping he'd see what she was trying to tell him. "I ended up going off with one of the guys. I don't know why. He'd been chatting me up and I…"

It sounded so bad, put this way, it sounded terrible, she knew it did. She'd been Barakan. Barakan enough to know she shouldn't have been there, shouldn't have had a drink, shouldn't have left the room with any man. Ever. "It got out of control."

She frowned hard, remembering, but not wanting to remember.

"Out of control?" he repeated.

She swallowed, nodded.

A long, awkward silence followed. "Did you have sex with him?"

He wasn't going to understand, was he? He wouldn't believe she'd been forced...

Men, especially Barakan men, always put the blame back on the woman. She felt absolutely heartsick. Her chest burned, heart on fire.

"Did you have sex with him?" Kalen repeated.

Hot, cold, Keira licked her lower lip. "I—"

He didn't let her answer. "What party was this, Keira?"

He was angry. His voice vibrated with fury. She shook her head, her long hair tumbling across her bare arm. She couldn't speak, not with her throat squeezing closed.

"Was this my party, Keira? The one thrown for me when I returned from London?"

He knew...

Her eyes watered. She nodded, speechless.

He left the bed, stalked away and then turned back to face her. "You were the one."

The disgust in his voice shattered her.

"I've heard all about you," he said, grabbing a

clean robe from the closet. "For months you were the talk of the town."

"Kalen—"

"Your party *friend* bragged about bedding you. He boasted about what you'd given him. Freely. Eagerly." Kalen's jaw jutted. His chest rose and fell with each huge livid breath. "You were insatiable."

No. Tears filled her eyes. No, no, it wasn't like that at all. But the protest was trapped inside her, the protest was lodged where words didn't go.

He looked at her so long, with so much judgment in his eyes that she felt part of her shrivel up and die.

"Who are you?" he demanded.

"You know me, Kalen."

"No. You're a mass of contradictions and even the contradictions contradict each other."

She swallowed. The corner of her mouth twitched, her features frozen. She could afford to be calm now. She'd seen his true colors. Knew how he felt.

It was over. Even if he hadn't said the words, she knew. It was over for her, too.

Kalen paced the length of the bedroom. "I can't believe it. Can't believe what you're telling me."

She simply looked at him, no emotions left. He

could talk, he could rage, he could say whatever he wanted. He was just like the others…

Just like the rest.

He made a hoarse sound, half despair, half rage. "Do you know how many times I heard the story of that night? Do you have any idea how many men know what was done with you…to you…?" His voice faded away, but not the incredulity. His shock hung there in the room, heavy and dark between them.

"But they don't know it's me," she said quietly, so shut down now she felt like she was on automation.

He swore. Violently. Bitterly. "But *I* do."

The longest twenty-four hours. Had it only been a day? Keira wondered wearily.

Had it only been twenty-four hours since she told Kalen what happened?

She was back in London. He'd put her on a plane so fast it had made her head spin. She couldn't even speak as he packed her bag for her. "It's better you go," he said, dumping her things into a soft leather suitcase.

She watched him dumbly, everything so dead inside her. "Go where?"

He gestured carelessly, refusing to look her in the eye. "Back to London—"

"I'd prefer to go home."

"London is home."

"No, that's your home. Mine is in Dallas. That's where I live." She had to choke back tears. "That's where I want to go now."

"We have to settle things first."

"Like what?"

"Our marriage, for one."

Ah. The legal issues. She tried to smile, tried to be cool, careless, callous but it was impossible. "We can't just settle that now?"

He zipped the leather bag closed. "No. I'm too angry. I need time. Space. You probably do, too."

But she didn't. She needed love, tenderness, kindness. She didn't need time. Or space.

He didn't care, though, did he?

She remained numb on the flight back to London, numb in the limousine, numb even as she unpacked her small suitcase in the bedroom of the penthouse apartment.

She'd worn little in Baraka but simple cotton robes, and those she never wanted to see again. The only gown she wanted to keep was her wedding dress. It wasn't particularly elaborate, just a column of ivory silk embroidered with gold and silver at the cuffs and hem. But she'd felt beautiful in the dress. Exotic. Mysterious.

Keira hung the dress up, smoothed the delicate

silk. She could feel the sadness building, the sorrow hot and heavy behind her eyes. But she wouldn't cry. Tears would only hurt worse.

If she cried she was acknowledging what she lost those years ago. She'd be facing the shame that couldn't come to light. If she'd been able to talk about the incident once...just once...would it have helped at all? Would she be different today?

Would she and Kalen be together today?

The days passed without word from Kalen. And every day she woke, wondering, would he call? Would he send word?

More importantly, she wanted to know what he intended to do. Was he going to divorce her? Ask for a legal separation? How did he plan on handling this?

It had been a week since she'd been put on a plane for London. A week where she couldn't eat, couldn't sleep, couldn't keep her emotions in check. She'd cried herself sick on more than one occasion.

How could Kalen think the worst of her?

How could he be so heartless? So cruel?

Because that's who he is, she told herself, pacing the penthouse living room restlessly, feeling like an exotic bird in a gilded cage. He does what he wants, when he wants. He's always been this way.

Like this penthouse, for example.

He'd brought her here not because she'd asked, not because she'd wanted an apartment of her own, but because it suited him.

Him.

And yes, it was luxurious, and boasted splendid views of the Thames, Big Ben and Parliament.

From nearly every room in the apartment she could see Tower Bridge, the barges, the tourists queuing up for the next trip down the famous river.

She could see the sun set and the lights of the city glimmer to life. She could see the moon rise high over the cityscape, watch the lights in the other high-rise flats switch off late at night as people went to bed, and still she was alone.

Keira walked past the baby grand piano, a black glossy bridge between two oversized corner windows and her fingertips trailed across the smooth paint, glossy slick beneath her skin.

What she wanted—needed—was to see Kalen again. She couldn't imagine living without him.

But she couldn't imagine he'd think so badly of her, either.

Did she love him, or hate him?

And if she hated him, why was she so desperate to be near him? Why did she crave the scent of his skin? The warmth when he dipped his head to kiss her hello? The hard, possessive light in his gold eyes?

Was this just lust? Sex? Animal attraction?

Was that what held her in his thrall? Even now she could feel the way he touched her, the brush of his lips across hers, the way his mouth shot torrents of feeling through her, daggers of sensation spilling from her belly into her veins…

She'd read about men like Kalen in her teenage romances, men that were tall, dark, invariably mysterious. She'd loved the idea of an exotic man sweeping her away from her ordinary world, sweeping her into the fantasy world her mother insisted didn't exist, the world her mother had taken such pleasure in dismissing, criticizing, condemning. And that man had been Kalen Nuri.

But men, as her mother had tried to teach her, are not storybook heroes.

Men do not save the day.

Men—

The doorbell rang, interrupting Keira's thoughts. He was here.

Her stomach came to life with a thousand dragonflies.

The butler appeared and Keira nodded, dragonflies taking wing as the serious gray-suited butler opened the door.

Kalen entered, handed his coat to the butler and then the butler was gone, leaving them alone.

She remained next to the piano, her left hand resting on the keyboard cover and yet she had eyes only for him.

Dark, so very dark and so very tall. His golden gaze rested on her, his expression pensive, more brooding than usual.

She needed to say something, greet him, but what? How?

Legally she was his wife. But emotionally she felt discarded. Abandoned. It was the worst feeling in the world. "Hello." Her voice came out deep, husky.

"Mesa l-khir," he answered. Good evening.

His greeting suddenly reminded her too vividly of their days in the desert together, their camel caravan, their nights sleeping in the tent, and that one dawn, where pink and yellow light touched the tent and Kalen had finally made love to her...

When he'd finally made her his.

It had been the most amazing morning of her life.

"A drink?" she asked, tears suddenly hot and gritty in the back of her eyes and nervously she rubbed at the piano with two fingers. Don't cry... don't cry...

His eyes narrowed, his expression enigmatic. "Is that what I need?"

She pressed harder on the piano. She didn't know what he needed, didn't know what they were doing here in the first place.

They'd been brought together by the threat Ahmed Abizhaid posed to the Sultan and his family. Kalen had been determined to keep her father from forming an alliance with Abizhaid…three weeks later, she was Kalen's wife and Abizhaid was dead.

What did Kalen propose to do with her now?

"It's been a week," she said simply, not knowing where else to begin.

"I needed time to think."

Ah. She felt her lips curve but it was a protective response. On the inside pain flickered through her, a radius of hurt that just went on and on.

"Do you know what hell is?" she asked, her voice pitched low. She stood at the window, looking out over the city, her gaze riveted to the illuminated London Eye. The ferris wheel that could take you to the top, let you see everything, that was larger than life itself.

The Eye.

"What's hell?"

"It's being caught in a lie you can never escape. It's being trapped with secrets that are an endless source of shame."

Her words were greeted by silence but she knew she wasn't alone. Knew he hadn't left the room. He was standing behind her, waiting, watching, listening.

He wanted her to continue talking. He wanted... more...

But that was the hell. She could go just so far, up to the line, to that place she didn't dare cross over. Because it had been kept buried so long she didn't even know how to access what had happened. She'd denied it, refused to acknowledge it, wouldn't let herself think or feel it and after six years it might not have ever been.

Maybe it hadn't even happened.

Maybe it was just a relic of a dream, something not good, but also not real.

"It's not a place, either. It's a state of being. A state without grace."

She turned, folded her arms across her chest, smiled tightly, mockingly, mocking herself. Dallas Cowboy cheerleader, beauty queen, bride of a sheikh, wife of the Ouaha Sultan.

And it meant nothing. Absolutely nothing if the one man she loved, the one man she needed, the one man she craved didn't respect her.

"I can't live without grace," she added, her gaze lifting, meeting his. "And then in this past week— the longest week of my life—I realized God would never deny me grace. God isn't ashamed of me." She took a quick breath. "And I'm not ashamed of me, either." It was true.

She didn't care what anyone else thought of her. She didn't care what Kalen thought of her, although Kalen had been the catalyst for the change.

It took her father's threat, the forced marriage, the wretched breaking of her heart, but finally she'd come to terms with her past.

What had happened had been years ago.

What had happened had been just one night—an hour at most—sixty minutes, maybe even forty, fifty—and it hadn't killed her.

It hadn't sucked the life out of her, drained her, embalmed her.

She wasn't a mummy. She wasn't dead. Far from dead. Her needs had returned, reasserting themselves, screaming to life.

But it took Kalen Nuri to make her realize how much she wanted still. How much she wanted to live.

It took Kalen Nuri for the air to surge through her lungs again.

Just one look at him and she'd begun clawing desperately for what she'd forgotten. Love. Contact. Forgiveness. Compassion.

All she wanted now was a fresh start. A new life. A chance to get her slate wiped clean.

"I didn't have sex with the man at your party," she said, lifting her chin. But the words still weren't easy to get out. Her throat felt tight, constricted. "I was assaulted. Sexually."

"Keira—"

"No. Let me finish. You never let me finish in Ouaha, and I was so hurt, so horrified by what you said—by what you believed—that I couldn't defend myself. That I didn't defend myself."

Her eyes burned and she frowned hard, focusing on the vase of flowers sitting on the piano, hoping to hold the tears back. "But that's the last time I accept an insult from you, or anyone else. Because I do deserve better, and I do deserve more.

"The night of your party I was attacked, assaulted." It was a battle to get the words out. They were the most awful words she knew, words that clumped in her throat, blocked the air, made her feel as if she were choking. Nearly as agonizing as the night the stranger had locked her in the room and taken her life from her. "I was brutally raped—" she took a rough breath "—and you were the first man I've been with since that night."

Trembling with exhaustion and emotion, she wanted to sit down, but first she had to finish, had to say the rest that burned in her heart, that weighed on her mind. "You said last week you needed time and space. Well, I've had time and space, too, and it's made me realize that I've been wronged again."

"Keira—"

"I'm not going to apologize, if that's what you want. I refuse to apologize for what was done to me. And I refuse to apologize for not being innocent when we married. I have carried too much shame for something I did not choose. I have suffered in silence for years, and Kalen, I will not suffer anymore."

Silence greeted her anguished words, the elegant living room deathly still.

"Forgive me," he said.

"That's all you have to say?"

The heaviest silence weighted the room, the silence an insurmountable wall between them.

His dark head inclined, his face half-averted. "I was wrong."

"It took you seven days to realize you were wrong?"

"No. It took me all of a minute to realize I was wrong. And six days, twenty-three hours and fifty-nine minutes to hunt down the bastard who hurt you."

"Yet you let me think the worst."

He looked at her, his expression tormented. "I didn't know you'd think the worst."

"How cruel can you be?" She spit the words out.

"You were awful. You were cold. You were harsh and judgmental—" She drew a deep breath. But he hadn't just judged her. He'd pulled away, sent her away, physically removed himself.

"That's not what I was feeling."

"But how was I to know? You didn't say anything kind. You didn't reach for me. Didn't touch me. Made no attempt to reassure me."

"I'm sorry."

She shook her head, undone, overwhelmed. He'd never understand what she'd been through. "What were you thinking?"

His hard features shifted, revealing an inner struggle. "Revenge."

Typical man! Tears filled her eyes. "You let me think I was bad. Irredeemable." Her voice broke. *"Unforgivable."*

"No."

"Unlovable."

He extended a hand toward her. "Come to me."

"I can't. Not now. Not again."

"Keira."

"I loved you."

"And I love you."

She lifted a hand, shielded her face, unwilling to let him see how raw the pain was, how deeply he'd hurt her. "But that's past tense."

"Not for me."

His voice pitched so low, rumbled through her. She shuddered, squeezed her hands into fists. "I want out of this marriage."

He didn't answer. Brutal emotion rose within her. He had to let her go. He had to give her freedom. She couldn't stay with a man who didn't understand...who wouldn't understand. She needed loyalty, fidelity, honor, respect...

She deserved that much.

She deserved more.

"Please, Keira." Kalen's deep voice sounded like sandpaper, rough, a grate of sound. "Do not judge me so harshly. I didn't realize...didn't think..." His voice drifted to silence, the silence stretched.

He tried again, features twisting, golden gaze revealing an agony of feeling. "I forget how Western you are, Keira. I forget you have suffered, forget that you cannot read my mind...know my thoughts. I see now how badly I have hurt you. I didn't know, didn't realize you needed me with you, not chasing after justice."

"Justice would have been your love."

"But you have that. Unquestionably. Unconditionally."

She felt the thick wall around her heart crack. It hurt, the pain deep, long, almost as if her ribs were being stretched apart.

Looking away, she stared sightlessly across the

room, trying to keep her expression blank, trying to keep from letting the tears fill her eyes. "Did you find him? The one that hurt me?"

"Yes."

Her laugh was shaky. "Is he still alive?"

"Barely."

Keira didn't know where to look, didn't know what to think. Kalen was here. He'd apologized. He'd said he'd gone after the bad guy...

It wasn't right.

He wasn't supposed to be that kind of man. He wasn't supposed to be larger-than-life, other-worldly. She exhaled in a short painful breath, her chest tight, muscles seizing. Kalen Nuri was not her mystery, her fantasy, her dream.

"But that's heroic," she said, fighting to keep her emotions under lock and key. "Chivalrous. You don't do chivalry, remember?"

"I guess there must be a little English blood in me somewhere."

"So seven years after the fact you go to avenge my honor?"

"I would have done it that night if I'd known."

"But I was no one then—"

"You were Keira al-Issidri. The most beautiful girl I'd ever seen."

She never thought there'd be anyone out there who'd understand her, or the things she wanted.

She'd given up on the girlish dreams of heroes and prince charming.

But listening to Kalen, she felt the worst kind of hope and hope was the last thing she wanted to feel.

Hope would lead to further disappointment. Far better to want nothing, wish for nothing.

"I can't do this anymore, Kalen. I still want out." Her hands shook and she balled them into fists on top of the piano. "I want to go back to Dallas."

"It will be hard for us to live a normal life, *laeela,* if we're living on two different sides of the Atlantic."

"A normal life for me is a life without you."

He was silent a long moment, so long that Keira turned her head, looked at him. His brow was deeply creased. His jaw flexed with repressed emotion.

"I will not divorce you," he said at length. "I can't. I care too much—"

"You don't care!" She left the piano, approached him, her body trembling with rage. "If you cared, you wouldn't have sent me away. If you cared, you would have called the moment you realized your mistake. If you cared, you wouldn't have broken my heart like that!"

"My heart was broken, too."

She exhaled in a whoosh of pain. "I saw your

face. I saw how you looked at me. You were disgusted—"

"I was shocked."

"At me."

"At what you'd been through. You forget, I'd heard the stories, the boasting, and yet once I realized it was you in that room the night of the party, you with your big blue eyes and your innocence and your sweetness trapped with that buffoon—" He broke off, drew a ragged breath. "I could think of nothing but murder. I planned to kill him."

CHAPTER THIRTEEN

SHE sat down abruptly on the arm of the white linen slipcovered sofa.

"That's why I sent you away so quickly." He continued talking in that hard, unyielding voice, the one that conveyed danger as well as retribution. "I had to get you to London, get you to safety, before I committed my act of violence."

She didn't know what to say, couldn't think of a thing. She stared numbly at him, and he stared right back. His gaze was so steady. No fear anywhere in his eyes. No remorse, either. Just confidence. Endless confidence. The man ruled life. Life did not rule him.

"And I would have killed him but Sheikh Tair wouldn't let me."

"He was there?"

"He was my witness." The corner of Kalen's mouth lifted. "In case I went too far."

She pressed a hand to her middle, queasy, heartsick. She knew Kalen too well to know he was not being ruthlessly honest. "Will you be punished?"

"By whom? My brother? Your father?"

"My father doesn't know."

"He does now. I gave him bloody hell for putting you through what he did. For making your childhood a living hell."

"It wasn't that bad, Kalen."

"You were lonely, and alone, and I deeply regret adding more pain and suffering to your life."

"Kalen—"

"I love you, *laeela*. I love you with every breath I take. I love you with every thought I think. I love you more than I've loved anyone and the fact that I have inflicted more pain staggers me. Shames me."

Wretched tears filled her eyes and she covered her face with her hands.

"I love you so much," he added quietly, "that I will move to Dallas with you. I will live in your house with you. I will drive you personally to your football games so you can dance for sixty thousand strangers in your little white outfit."

Her flood of tears turned into a burst of laughter. *"Allah ister!"* she cried in protest. *God save us!* "You can't be serious. You, in Dallas, in my house? Kalen. You're not just a sheikh...you're a sultan! How will I explain you to my neighbors?"

He grimaced and yet the expression in his eyes

gentled, the golden depths warm and kind. "Very, very carefully."

He was impossible. He was making everything so difficult. She laughed, and cried, and threw up her hands in disgust. "I'm a mess. Completely destroyed."

"You've done the same thing to my heart."

"*La*. No—"

"*Iya*. Yes."

And sitting there, on the arm of the sofa, she felt a wave of hope. Hope matched by desire. Hot, sharp, fierce desire. The desire to be real again. The desire to be a woman again, Kalen's woman. The desire for Kalen's strength, Kalen's heat, Kalen's possession.

But could she trust him?

Could she possibly forgive him?

He must have read the indecision in her eyes because some of the warmth faded from his expression, his features slowly closing.

He looked like the old Sheikh Nuri. Detached. Distant. Cynical.

She'd hurt him, she realized. She'd rejected him when he was reaching out to her. But she needed time. She needed to think. "Maybe we should talk tomorrow? It's late. We're both probably quite tired—"

"I can't leave. Not yet."

She felt his resistance, that formidable strength and iron will which made him who he was. But she'd changed. She'd grown, matured, found her own footing. The only way they could come together, be together, was as equals. And she needed time. "I won't be pressured. Not by you. Not anymore."

He smiled suddenly, rather ruefully. "It's always worked before."

She spluttered and then when he laughed, she understood he'd been teasing her. She made a face at him. "I've changed, Kalen. You better change, too."

"I agree." And there was nothing teasing in his somber answer.

Keira studied him a long moment, saw the deep creases at the edge of his eyes, the grooves paralleling his mouth. He looked tired. This hadn't been an easy week for him, either. "You can't bully people to get what you want," she said softly. "You have to be fair. You have to respect others."

"I do. As long as the Sultan's safety—and your safety—are not compromised."

"I'm not part of the equation."

"*Laeela,* you are the equation. You are my heart, my soul, my lover, my wife—"

"First wife," she interrupted in disgust.

A glimmer returned to his eyes. "Only wife."

"You say that now," she answered darkly.

He laughed appreciatively, shook his head. "If you're this difficult as *jamal,* what will you be like as *shayla?*"

Her jaw dropped open. "You didn't just refer to me as a pregnant camel, did you?"

He laughed again, a deep husky sound rumbling from his chest. Keira had never heard him laugh so deeply, or so long. He was laughing because he was happy.

Happy. Because he was with her. Because he was teasing her. Because...

He loved her.

She knew it, knew it as surely as she knew her own name. Her eyes watered. "Maybe we could go out for a bit...grab some dinner?"

He started toward her, and then held back. She saw his hand clench. He wanted to touch her, but he was afraid. Sheikh Kalen Nuri afraid. Her heart turned inside out. The man who'd spent his life masking his emotions was revealing far too much.

"I'll make reservations," he said.

She nodded, eyes burning, heart on fire. "I'll go shower and change."

The restaurant was tucked into a private club, the interior dark, the walls shades of blue and green. A live band played, a popular group visiting from the States and playing a few small gigs in London hotspots.

Even though Keira liked the band, tonight she didn't give a damn about music. She had eyes only for Kalen. But then he suddenly stood, reached for her hand. "Dance?"

It wasn't really a question, though, and she put her hand in his, let him pull her slowly to her feet.

She'd been calm during dinner, felt reasonably controlled sipping her after dinner drink but all that changed the moment Kalen drew her into his arms on the dance floor.

Something happened when he touched her. It was like touching a live-wire—hot, sharp, explosive. She jumped inwardly, a jolting of the senses.

Keira's head jerked up, her gaze lifting to search his, wondering if he felt what she felt, or if it was all in her head.

But no, she corrected as his warmth seeped into her, this attraction…sensation…wasn't something she imagined. Something really did happen when she was with him. She changed. She came alive.

Like now. What she felt confused her, over-whelmed her. Her skin was so sensitive she could have been burning, simmering, everything in her growing tighter, warmer. Her face felt tingly and hot. Her breathing felt constricted. Her body wasn't cooperating.

She'd danced for thousands of people in the American football stadiums but she'd never felt as aware of herself as she did now.

And here she had the attention of only one man.

His dark head tipped. She felt his scrutiny. When he looked at her, he seemed to see everything.

His mouth touched her temple. Icy heat rushed through her, shivers of sensation raced up her spine. "So responsive," he murmured, lips brushing her cheek and she trembled against him, dazzled by the sensation, by the exquisite flood of pleasure. "I've never met anyone so sensitive."

But she wasn't so sensitive. It was him. He did this to her, this was all him, the power of his effect on her. "It's you," she whispered, feeling her breasts grow heavy, her insides tighten, her body hum with desire. "I'm sure everyone is this way with you."

"That would be convenient."

She didn't know how to answer that and he took advantage of her silence to urge her closer, so close that she could feel his thigh between her own, the hard flat muscles of his abdomen, the width of his chest.

Every shift of her hips brought her into more intimate contact with him. His hips were lean, his thighs muscular, and the cut of his elegant trousers revealed more than concealed the fact that his body was aroused. Powerfully so.

The ridge of his erection teased her skin, his long rigid shaft pressing from the inside of her thigh to her lower belly.

Heat prickled through her. Her nipples puckered tighter. Each breath felt more labored. They might as well have been naked, she thought, shocked as well as more than a little bit awed. He was so physical, so comfortable with the physical, while she felt like an absolute amateur.

"You're trembling," he said, his voice pure male seduction in her ear.

"You're doing crazy things to me."

"That's good."

"Or bad, depending on the way you look at it."

"And how do you look at it?"

She felt the weight of the past week return, the hurt and fear, and suddenly she didn't want to be dancing anymore, didn't want to be this close. Their bodies just confused the issue. What they needed was logic.

Discipline.

Common sense.

"Could we just head home?" she asked, drawing back, looking up into his face.

His expression was shuttered. She could see nothing in his eyes. "Of course."

They settled into the back of the limousine and the only sound was that of cars passing by, and the odd voice of the pedestrian outside.

"I know you never planned on marrying me, Kalen." Her voice broke the heavy silence.

"Not true. You're the only one I've ever considered marrying."

"But you didn't want to marry."

"I suppose that's true."

She swallowed around the lump in her throat. Her fingers worked the leather seat. "Marriage is that miserable?"

He laughed shortly, mockingly. "Marriage requires dependability. Reliability. I'm neither."

"You're afraid you'll…cheat?"

He laughed again but this time he sounded tired. Almost resigned. "It's not an issue of fidelity. But of longevity."

In the dim light of the car she saw him close his eyes, press two fingers to the bridge of his nose.

"I'm a sheikh," he said after a moment. "Son of a sultan, brother to a sultan, and I've inherited a legacy of unrest and bloodshed. The men in my family do not live long. Nearly half die violently. My grandmother was widowed at forty-seven. I'll never forget her grief. She was devastated by my grandfather's death—we all were—but she was inconsolable." He dropped his hand, opened his eyes, looked at her. "I never wanted to risk hurting someone that way. Didn't want to cause such grief."

Impulsively Keira reached out to him, touched his forearm. "But you don't even live in Baraka. You haven't for years."

"And yet I haven't left Baraka, either." He reached for her hand, lifted it from his sleeve, and turning her hand over placed a kiss in the middle of her palm. "I oversee Baraka's Secret Service, the agency responsible for protecting the Sultan and his family. I would drop everything for Malik and his family. I'd give my life for him, or his children."

She heard the fierce edge in his voice, his tone quiet and yet determined. Unexpected tears pricked her eyes. "But of course you would. I'd expect nothing less."

"And as your husband...the father of your children...it wouldn't eat away at you, my loyalty to the Sultan? You wouldn't see it as a conflict of interest?"

It scared her to think that he might be hurt, but she understood, too. "I might only be half-Barakan, but when I look at you I don't see the wealthy sheikh with the expensive toys and apartments. I see the man that can live simply in a tent, that prefers the company of Berber tribesmen to noisy clubs."

Her voice dropped, deepened. "When I look at you I can only see the man with the desert sun in his eyes and the desert sand in his veins. You're Kalen Nuri, second son to the Sultan Roman Nuri, grandson to the martyred Sultan Sherif Nuri. You can only be who you are designed to be."

"And what was I designed to be?" Kalen asked coolly, but Keira wouldn't bite at the bait.

"Great." Her lips curved. Her heart ached. "You are truly great."

The interior light suddenly flicked on flooding the back of the car with bright yellow light. Kalen stared at her, his features drawn, his expression so hard his cheekbones looked jagged beneath the golden skin. "Great?"

His intimidating expression would have once terrified her but now she knew it was a cover for the emotions that ran so deep within him. "You're fearless. A born leader."

"A leader to whom? A leader to what?"

"The people. The Berbers. In Oahua, and Baraka." The savage emotion inside her chest made it increasingly difficult to speak. "And I've known all along that you'd sacrifice yourself for your family. I've known from the beginning I might not have forever with you. And I've accepted that. Made peace with that. It's probably one of the reasons I love you as much as I do."

His gaze never wavered from her face. "You still love me?"

Her shoulders lifted, fell. "I've always loved you. Foolish me. I don't know how not to."

He turned his head, closed his eyes, but not before she saw the sheen of emotion.

Back at the penthouse, Kalen scooped her into his arms the moment the door shut, carrying her to the bedroom.

He dropped her gently in the middle of the bed, and followed her onto it, settling his weight over her. His kisses were deep, drugging. He slid his hands into her hair, fingers tangling in the black silky strands and held her still.

He kissed her as though he couldn't get enough, kissed her like a man parched, starving, a man in need of life.

Of love.

Keira gave herself over to his demands, realizing he needed her just as much—if not more—than she needed him.

He stripped her of her clothes, and then took off his own, and once naked, he stretched out over her, his long muscular limbs so warm, so tantalizing against hers.

Holding her hands in one of his, he kissed his way from her lips to her chin, down the side of her neck to the collarbone. She squirmed against him, hips lifting, legs twisting between his. The feel of his mouth on her skin wasn't enough, not when she wanted—needed—him.

But instead of giving in to her silent demands, he lowered his head over her breast, licking the taut nipple up, down, licking to madden the nerves but not to satisfy. Whimpering, she caught one of Kalen's thighs between hers and clamped tight.

Kalen wouldn't be rushed. Defiantly he kissed the fullness of her breast, kissed the sensitive skin beneath, the softness at the sides, kissed the slope, the hollow between before taking the aching nipple in his mouth again and sucking hard.

Her insides clenched, a spasm of feeling, and then another. The harder he sucked, the tighter the contractions became. She felt so hot, so wet, shamelessly needy.

He had to touch her soon, had to put his hand between her legs, had to relieve her of the torment, the pressure building, the aching tension that wouldn't be eased.

And then his hand moved down her belly, fingers trailing slowly over her flat tummy, the mound of Venus, through dark curls to the slick delicate folds of her sex.

He caressed her, parting the inner lips to test her readiness. She was ready. She felt positively ripe, her body humming, hot, fierce, wanting just him.

The need for him, for all of him, the need to be taken by him, held by him, controlled every thought and impulse. Her lips clung to his, her heart hammered hard in her ears, the pounding of her pulse, the heavy thudding in her veins louder than any words.

The only thing that would save her now was him.

She felt her body tremble against his, felt the huge hunger grow, swelling by the second, blooming into full orange and scarlet roses, overblown, savagely beautiful. Nothing controlled, or understated. Just wild desperate emotion. Just untempered passion. The passion of one who has waited her whole life to have a moment of this. Touch. Pleasure. Sensation. Acceptance.

"No more," she whispered, as his finger slipped in and out of her. "No more foreplay. I just want you inside me."

She nearly cried out as he entered her, stunned by the thick fullness of him. She'd forgotten how big he was, had forgotten how hot and satin his shaft felt inside of her.

She held her breath as she struggled to take him all, her body almost aching at the stretched sensation. It was wonderful. It was also overwhelming. But then her body adjusted, the pressure easing as she accepted him.

"*Laeela,*" he murmured against her ear. "My wife, my love."

Slowly he began to move inside her. Long, slow strokes, long sure strokes. The intense sensation caught her, transported her.

It wasn't sex. It was a dance—a dance of blindness, a dance of silence, a dance that had nothing to do with music or color, shape or form. It was just a dance of skin. Every nerve was awake, every sense stirred. All she had to do was close her eyes, and feel, and follow the unspoken rhythm.

And she did. She gave herself up, gave herself over, and he in turn gave her exquisite pleasure.

It took forever to regroup from the shattering climax. He'd kept her at a peak of sensation so long her muscles and nerves couldn't seem to recover. Her thoughts were just as scattered.

But eventually she did pull together, and while her skin still glowed pink and damp, and her body still felt blissfully boneless, she forced herself to lean over him, and turn on the bedside lamp.

"What are you doing?" he asked, stroking her arm, her shoulder, the line of her back as she leaned over him.

"I have to see you," she said, remaining propped on her elbow.

"Why?"

But she didn't answer right away. Instead she looked at him with pain and wonder.

Kalen Nuri. The ache inside her intensified.

All those chance sightings over the years… And then the waiting between glimpses for the next chance sighting…

She used to wait six months, sometimes a year for one of those sightings. And each glimpse was exquisitely brief.

Moments…seconds…

The side of the face, the back of the head, the limousine driving past.

Each time she'd stop, frozen, entranced. Everything would still, her heart and her breath, her mind, her body, her life. The past wasn't real. The future would never come.

Just one moment and she could be someone, something else.

Just one moment and she was free, airborne, soaring with hope, emotion, new dreams. He was gorgeous. He was big. Strong. He was so far apart from her world, so very removed and there was no way to close the void, no way to get near, no way to even find out that which she wanted, no way to find peace or happiness.

There was just that one moment to hope, to believe.

One second.

And yet in one second she'd lived more than most had lived in years.

In those scattered seconds she'd lived, died, dreamed.

In those scattered seconds brought together, lined up, ordered, collected, she'd escaped her body, escaped her shame and she'd been free.

Free to feel. Free to love.

"Tell me," Kalen said, clasping her face between his hands. He drew her face down to his, brushed his lips across hers. The kiss was tantalizing and sweet. "What do you see?"

What did she see? How did she answer that?

Her eyes burned. She blinked. She fought back the threat of tears. "I see my heart."

"Your heart," he repeated quietly.

She nodded. Bit hard into her lower lip. "You own it."

"I am very blessed."

"But if you should leave—"

He cut her off with another kiss, his fingers warm against her cheekbones, his thumbs stroking the soft warm skin. "I'd never leave you. I could never leave you. Only death could take me from you."

She pressed her brow to his. "Don't say such a thing."

"It's true. I love few people, but those I love, I protect with my life." He pressed a kiss to her temple, the arched wing of her eyebrow, the corner of her mouth. "You know I would give my life for you in an instant. Without question."

"It's not what I'd ever want."

"But it's what you deserve. Real love. Lasting love. Someone to fight for you when need be—"

"No." She covered his mouth, her lips drinking from his, drawing his breath into her body and mouth. Long moments later she lifted her head. "Thank you, Your Excellency, but no. I think I've finally learned to fight my own battles, to fight for myself."

"Battles are dirty business."

A wry smile tugged at her mouth. "Perhaps. But I'm not afraid anymore."

"Not afraid to fight?" His rough voice was warmed by tenderness. "You must have some Berber blood in you, *laeela*."

She laughed. "No, darling. I've just had you in me."

He suddenly shifted, catching her in his arms and rolling her onto her back. His body moved against her, his strong thighs parting her knees and settling between.

She gasped at the feel of him against her. He was already hard, rigid, and the feel of his erection pressing against her still sensitive skin sent shivers through her.

His head dipped aggressively, his mouth covered the hollow in her throat, his tongue snaking wet circles on her hot skin. She writhed beneath him, legs opening wider, hips arching, desperate for relief.

She wanted him, wanted him more than she'd ever wanted anything and she clasped his hips, slid her hands across his tight firm buttocks, the muscle dense beneath her fingers. "Kalen…"

Her groan was cut off by the surge of his body entering hers.

"Mine," he said, pushing forward, filling her, stretching her, answering her tremendous need. "Mine, you are mine now and always." And as he thrust forward, filling her completely, he touched his lips to hers. "Just as I give you, *laeela,* all of me."

She clung to him as he began to move, no slow leisurely lovemaking this time, but he drove hard, fast, each surge of his lean hips conveying stark need and urgency.

Her eyes closed, her body clung to his, her legs wrapped around his hips to hold him deeper, to satisfy the need that seemed impossible to appease.

The friction of his body in hers, the hot electric awareness, the spiral of desire urged them on. Their hunger for each other set the tempo. Their emotions heightened the delight.

Miracles did happen, Keira thought. Dreams did come true.

The coiling of pleasure inside her began. He felt the tension within her, as well as her instinctive resistance.

His thrusts quickened, each stroke pushing her closer to the edge. She wasn't going to be able to hold back much longer. Helplessly she arched against him, her body straining, muscles tight. And then she was exploding, coming apart in waves of shuddering pleasure, the colors in her head like the colors of the desert—intense reds, gold, crimson, ochre, her body as hot as the sand beneath the sun, her body hastening like the shifting sands.

He kissed her as she shattered, kissed her as her fierce climax brought him fulfillment, too.

Tears of joy slipped from beneath her lashes as Kalen held her shuddering body against him, holding her through the fierce storm of passion and emotion.

When reality exceeds expectations…

When fact is more interesting than fiction…

"Are you okay?" he asked, wiping a stray tear from her damp hair.

"Yes. I'm very okay." She burrowed closer, pressing in, skin to skin, heart to heart, life to life.

"Then why are you crying, *laeela?*"

"*Ouaha,*" she answered. "I've finally found my own oasis. My oasis is with you."

WEB_M&B_RTL3 LP

Discover Pure Reading Pleasure with

Visit the Mills & Boon website for all the latest in romance

🌹 **Buy** all the latest releases, backlist and eBooks

🌹 **Find out** more about our authors and their books

🌹 **Join** our community and chat to authors and other readers

🌹 **Free** online reads from your favourite authors

🌹 **Win** with our fantastic online competitions

🌹 **Sign** up for our free monthly eNewsletter

🌹 **Tell us** what you think by signing up to our reader panel

🌹 **Rate** and review books with our star system

www.millsandboon.co.uk

 Follow us at twitter.com/millsandboonuk

 Become a fan at facebook.com/romancehq

Discover Pure Reading Pleasure with

MILLS &
BOON

Visit the Mills & Boon website for all
the latest in romance

❤ Buy all the latest
releases, backlist
and eBooks

❤ Join our community
and chat to authors
and other readers

❤ Win with our
fantastic online
competitions

❤ Tell us what you think
by signing up to our
reader panel

❤ Find out more
about our authors
and their books

❤ Free online reads
from your favourite
authors

❤ Sign up for our
free monthly
eNewsletter

❤ Rate and review
books with our star
system

www.millsandboon.co.uk

Follow us at twitter.com/millsandboonuk

Become a fan at facebook.com/romancehq